## 'Lilly, what the hell are you doing here?'

'I… um…' she stammered. 'I…could ask you the same.' Although she knew, of course, as he was holding the World Aid sign, down by his side now. 'World Aid sent me here.'

'This is no place for you,' he said, his eyes blazing down into hers. 'Are you mad? This place could go up in flames any day now.'

'You mean it's all right for you to put your life on the line, but not me?' she countered. Instinctively she wanted to go into Rafe's arms, to be held by him as she once would have been. In the past weeks he had never been out of her mind; now it was amazingly wonderful to see him in the flesh.

'Yes, I do mean that,' he said. 'When I last saw you, you were pretty vulnerable.'

'I'll manage,' she said, staring back at him challengingly.

**Rebecca Lang** trained to be a State Registered Nurse in Kent, England, where she was born. Her main focus of interest became operating theatre work, and she gained extensive experience in all types of surgery on both sides of the Atlantic. Now living in Toronto, Canada, she is married to a Canadian pathologist and has three children. When not writing, Rebecca enjoys gardening, reading, theatre, exploring new places, and anything to do with the study of people.

**Recent titles by the same author:**

THE SURGEON'S SECRET SON
THE BABY SPECIALIST
CHALLENGING DR BLAKE

# NURSE
# ON ASSIGNMENT

BY
REBECCA LANG

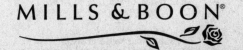

MILLS & BOON®

*First published in Great Britain 2005*
*Harlequin Mills & Boon Limited,*
*Eton House, 18-24 Paradise Road, Richmond, Surrey TW9 1SR*

© Rebecca Lang 2005

ISBN 0 263 84308 4

*Set in Times Roman 10½ on 13 pt.*
*03-0505-43062*

*Printed and bound in Spain*
*by Litografia Rosés, S.A., Barcelona*

# CHAPTER ONE

WHEN the front doorbell rang on the Sunday afternoon, Lilly Page was not expecting it.

She thought that maybe Rafe was home and had forgotten his key. Eagerly she flung open the door.

The two women who stood on the doorstep were not familiar to her. One of them was in early middle age, beautifully and expensively dressed, very attractive with dyed blonde hair, the other considerably older, but equally well dressed with understated elegance, heavily made up. For some reason that she could not have explained, Lilly felt a strange twinge of apprehension.

"Are you Lilly?" the younger woman asked, after appraising her quickly from head to toe.

"Yes," Lilly said, feeling mystified, yet with a deepening peculiar premonition of disaster. There was something insolent in the way the woman looked her over, as though she had every right to do so.

They were like two exotic birds that had escaped from a cage, Lilly thought, and found themselves in the wrong habitat. Behind them, parked on the street, Lilly could see a silver-grey sports car, a convertible. It seemed to ooze money and was equally out of place in the quiet street of reclaimed old houses in central Toronto.

"I'm Marie Neilson," the younger woman said, smiling slightly, obviously gratified at the reaction her words had had on Lilly. "And this is my mother, Anthea. I'm Rafe's stepmother."

As she looked back at them in surprise, Lilly had the feeling that Anthea was not the older woman's real name. It did not fit her, for all her surface veneer of wealth. There was a certain lack of ease in her, a crudeness.

"Oh," Lilly said, forcing a smile, "I'm afraid Rafe isn't in, he's at the hospital and on call this evening. He didn't say—"

"That's all right," Marie Neilson interrupted. "We knew he would be out. It's you we want to see. May we come in?"

"Me?" She stared back at them, looking from one to the other, aware of an unsubtle hostility in them. Then she remembered her manners. "Yes, do come in, then," she said, stepping back, pulling the door open wide to let them in.

They must have watched the house, she thought, before they had knocked on the door, to make sure that Rafe was out and she was in. Why?

As she preceded them to the sitting room, she had the sense that the cosy world of love, companionship and understanding that she shared with Rafe was being invaded. And she was frightened, although she could not have said why at that moment. They had created a cocoon for themselves, she and Rafe. When he had told her something about his family, that his parents had divorced when he had been fourteen years old, that his father had made a lot of money from oil, he had also told her that he had lived with his mother more than his father when he had been younger, although they were on good terms. All this went through her mind quickly as she speculated on why these women were there.

"Perhaps you'd like a drink?" she offered. "Tea? Or something cool?"

"No, we won't have anything, thank you," Marie Neilson said decisively, as she looked around her. "We want to talk to you. What we have to say won't take long. It's not exactly a social visit."

There was a certain faint snide and sneering quality to her words that Lilly—hyper-sensitive now to a hostility that seemed to emanate from them—assumed was just a prelude to an interview of sorts that was not going to be pleasant.

What was all this about? She resolved not to be intimidated in her own home by people who had essentially invited themselves in. Already she felt the obtrusiveness of their personalities; there was nothing graceful or gentle about either of them, as they eyed her like the proverbial hawks, unsmiling and calculating.

Theirs was not "old money", she suspected. Already

she could tell that they did not have what her mother would have called "breeding", essentially good manners, to go with it. Indeed, there was a brazen, proprietorial air about them as they entered, as though they had every right to do so and looked around them openly at the furnishings of the room, the pictures, the few framed photographs on a table, as though they themselves were invisible, or as though they were in a public gallery.

Now she recalled that Rafe had also told her how he had done his utmost, as a high school student, to get into medical school so that he would not have to go into the family business, as his father had expected him to do, as the only child.

Lilly was glad of the charm of the late Victorian house as she walked ahead into the sitting room, sparsely and simply furnished, which suited her and Rafe.

The two women watched her as their eyes darted quickly around the room. "Please, sit," Lilly offered, indicating the comfortable sofa. As they sat side by side, she sat opposite, feeling that this was to be an inquisition of sorts. Why would they come to see her when Rafe was out? "How can I help you?" she added.

"We'll get straight to the point," Marie Neilson said, leaning forward and clasping her hands in front of her, perfect with their bright red varnished nails. "We understand that you are pregnant. Rafe told his father and…I happened to overhear the telephone conversation.''

Taken aback, Lilly stared at them, momentarily speechless.

At that moment she recalled something else that Rafe had told her, that Marie had not been able to have children, a fact that his father had seriously regretted, and which he had not known prior to their marriage. Marie, the daughter of a wealthy family with ''new money'', had apparently pursued Rafe's father relentlessly after his divorce.

It had been Marie's father, a construction worker, who had made a lot of money from taking out mortgages on semi-derelict commercial buildings in unfashionable parts of downtown Toronto and turning them gradually into trendy loft flats, just before there had been a real-estate boom and gentrification of those areas.

That information, which Rafe had not made a big deal of, had more or less passed over her head at the time of his telling. Now it came back in full force. Not being mercenary herself, and sensing that Rafe was trying to put certain aspects of his childhood behind him, she had had the feeling at the time that it had very little, if anything, to do with her.

''Yes…I am pregnant,'' Lilly said, her voice high-pitched with nervousness, staring back at them, trying not to show her lack of ease. ''I don't see—'' The expression on the other woman's face was one of snide knowingness, which somehow made Lilly feel that she was in a position of disadvantage.

Again she was cut off. ''You know, of course, that Rafe is potentially a very wealthy young man, who will inherit a large part of the family fortune when his father dies?'' Marie stated.

''I—I didn't know,'' Lilly stammered. ''I am not privy to his father's will. Rafe and I have never discussed it. I know his father is in business of some sort—''

''Of course you knew!'' The older woman butted in for the first time, her steely, dark eyes on Lilly's face, without a hint of friendliness in them.

''What is all this about?'' Lilly demanded, her heart thudding from the shock of the other woman's rudeness. ''Rafe's an adult, he doesn't need you to…to speak for him, if that is what you're doing. As far as I know, his father is in good health. I…don't understand.''

''You must know that Rafe is a gentleman,'' the older woman went on. ''You must have known that he would offer to marry you, and then—bingo!—that great fortune would be yours.''

So that was why they were there. They assumed that she had become pregnant deliberately to trap Rafe for his money. The realization of it made her feel physically sick. Was it possible that he thought that, too?

A healthy anger came to her rescue. ''Would it?'' Lilly said, having swallowed the lump in her throat.

"I've never played bingo and I don't know the rules." Somehow the words and the courage to utter them had come to her. She kept her voice calm, not generally being disposed to rudeness. Out of character though it was, she had to defend herself.

"Don't give me that!" the other woman said brusquely, her voice rising. "You know the bloody rules of the game you're playing all right. I'm an intelligent woman. Don't think you can pull the wool over my eyes."

"Ma, take it easy," Marie murmured to her mother, who was now red in the face.

Shocked and oddly frightened, with a dawning sense of *déjà vu*, Lilly swallowed again nervously, and gathered together what she could of her courage. "Nothing was further from my mind," she said calmly and reasonably. "As you know, Rafe has been independent of his family for a long time. We…we've discussed the pregnancy and decided just to live together…as we are now."

"But for how long?" Marie said harshly. "With a child, you would eventually marry."

"I honestly don't know," Lilly said, more firmly. "Not necessarily. We haven't discussed the future much. We prefer to just live in the present for now. And I don't think that our private life is any of your business."

"'Just live in the present!'" Anthea parodied her words. "It's pretty obvious that you're a calculating little bitch, with not much money of your own.'' She gestured around the room. ''Otherwise you wouldn't be living like this, with next to nothing.''

''We like it that way,'' Lilly managed to get out, feeling cold with shock at the increasing, unprovoked hostility that confronted her. ''We love each other.''

''Love! Hah!'' the older woman said sarcastically. ''It's easy to profess love in your situation. Rafe can have any woman he wants, he doesn't have to settle for you. I reckon you're pretty vulnerable right now and see Rafe as a cash cow.''

''No! How dare you accuse me of that?'' Lilly stood up. ''It simply isn't true. I'd like you to leave now.'' Standing, she felt that she had a slight advantage. ''This is so…so Victorian. I can't believe you would come here to be abusive to me. What difference does it make to you who Rafe marries? He is not your son.''

''Let me tell you,'' Marie said, ''that if he marries you, we'll see to it that he is cut off without a cent. We have the utmost influence with his father.''

''Is that so?'' Lilly countered. ''It's of no interest to me, and I know that Rafe is quite capable of earning a living without any financial aid from anyone. I support myself, and shall continue to do so for as long as I can.''

In spite of her bravado, she heard a slight tremor in her own voice and found herself shivering, overwhelmed by a sense of unreality, as though she were taking part in a badly written play that had been insufficiently rehearsed. No one had called her a calculating little bitch before—it was a description that bore no relationship to her own reality.

"Rafe will get married one day," she went on, forcing her voice into reasonableness, when she really wanted to scream at them to get out. "How could you possibly stop him?"

"Yes, I expect he will marry," Marie said smoothly. "But not you. Not to someone who has so obviously trapped him into it. He needs a woman who will bring her own wealth to the marriage, to match his."

"Isn't that idea somewhat out of date?" Lilly managed to say.

"Be that as it may," Marie said, "it's what we want and expect."

"It isn't in your hands," Lilly said. "Rafe is a mature man, he'll make up his own mind."

"He's too young to be a father, it's not the right time for him," Anthea said.

So that was part of it, Lilly realized as she stared at the two women, who were still seated. Marie had been unable to have children, and they were not ready for another young Neilson to appear on the scene, to perhaps dilute the inheritance that they thought was rightfully theirs. Rafe's real mother had given birth to two more children by a man with whom she lived but had never married, so he was not an only child. Yet for the purposes of inheritance from his own father, he was the sole heir, the blood child. A grandchild, she could see now for the first time, would most likely be very welcomè to Rafe's father.

"We'll give you half a million dollars to give him up," Marie said smoothly.

"What?" Lilly said. "No! Are you mad?"

"One million," Anthea said.

"No! You don't seem to understand. We love each other. It has nothing to do with money."

"I doubt that he'll love you when he's been cut out of the family money," Rafe's stepmother said.

Lilly walked towards the door of the room, feeling suddenly more physically sick than ever, knowing that most of the colour had gone from her face.

The *déjà vu* feeling came again as she recalled with perfect clarity the sneering voice of a boy at her school when she had been little, saying to her, "You're white trash!" He had followed it up with, "You're trailer trash, you live in a trailer. Only stupid people and losers live in trailers."

For years she had thought that she had well and truly got over the experience, especially when she had qualified as a registered nurse, gained a university degree and gone on to get much interesting work experience. Now, as she prepared to get the women to leave her home, she knew that she had been irretrievably scarred by that childhood encounter, which seemed such a petty thing in itself. Even moving into the lovely old red brick mansion, somewhat run-down, in Albertstown, the cosy small town where she had spent the remainder of her childhood, had not erased the bitter memory of those months in the trailer, which had been forever changed by someone else's view.

That boy, all those years ago, had pricked the bubble of her innocent self-esteem and unconscious happiness in her family life. He had forced her to view it in another way, a way that he had imposed on her. This new verbal assault seemed to build on the old.

"Please, leave my house," she said with dignity, pausing in the doorway. "I advise you not to judge others by your own brand of morality. I've met Rafe's father, and his mother, and I don't think his father would be very influenced by two women who clearly do not have Rafe's best interests at heart. If he were planning what you suggest, to cut Rafe out of his will, I think he would come to see me himself. Goodbye."

To her surprise, the two women seemed struck dumb by her show of quiet dignity.

"Rafe and I have no plans to marry," she repeated, a tremble in her voice that she could not control. "Far from trapping him, I am the one who wishes to keep things just as they are. And if he decides he doesn't want to be with me, so be it."

As they went out, Lilly said, "Don't come here again unless you're invited to do so." With clumsy fingers she shut the door, turned the lock and put the chain on the door.

Back in the sitting room, which now seemed tainted

from the lingering presence of the two spiteful women, Lilly watched through the window as they retreated through the garden gate. Already she had a sense of unreality, as though the strange interview had been a figment of her imagination. Uncontrollable tears came to her eyes, and her hands, clasped tightly together, were shaking. A strange and total sadness had come over her, like a sense of mourning, and with a sharp insight she knew the encounter had taken her back to the past when she had been made to feel less than human, less of a worthy person in her own right.

The roar of the car engine outside seemed to mock her—trash, trash, trash! So clearly over the years the traumatic events of her childhood had become explicable to her, the chain of events that had made her vulnerable and had had an indelible effect on her.

First, her beloved father, whose absences with the army had infected the whole family with chronic anxiety, had been wounded in a war zone overseas. For an agonizing time of enforced helplessness they had not known whether he had been alive or dead, only that he had been wounded. Then he had surfaced in a hospital in Germany, where he had been taken after being airlifted out of Africa.

Although her mother must have been told the extent of his injuries, the children had not known fully until they had seen him come out of an airport, walking on a pair of crutches, minus part of a leg. Then had followed a period of uncertainty, when he had no longer been physically fit for military service. Then she had understood that he had been considered flawed, no longer a perfect specimen of manhood who could put his life on the line once again for his country and all the people in it.

Feeling sick, Lilly quickly walked out to the kitchen and leant over the sink, closing her eyes, supporting herself with both hands on the counter. Taking deep breaths, she tried to calm herself. She felt that her face was pale and clammy.

The taunting of the boy at school had not only mocked her, but had mocked her father and his effort, had mocked their suffering. It would have been all the same to the careless boy whether her father had lived or died; all he had been able to see had been that they were poor and lived in a trailer.

Then she began to walk around the house restlessly, hands clasped tightly, trying to make up her mind whether to call Rafe at work and tell him. A sense of being violated and invaded was strong.

Perhaps she had been right to think that Rafe was out of her league, as she had when she had first met him at the big teaching hospital where they both worked in the operating rooms, yet she realized now that she had never really thought that she could not choose a man she wanted, expect him to love her and maybe marry her. Even if she had not had the confidence for it, she did not think she was prohibited. Maybe, she considered now, there was a code for the super-rich that she could not be privy to. Perhaps you had to buy your way into their lives, and she did not qualify.

As time went by and she paced around the house aimlessly, she felt less and less like telling Rafe. Her first reaction had been to rush to the telephone, to call him at work. Then she had hesitated because he would most likely be in the middle of a case in the operating rooms and she would not be able to talk to him anyway.

What if she just left it? What could they do to her after all, the stepmother and step-grandmother? She didn't know how to tell him that they had offered her a million dollars to get out of his life. How sordid it all seemed, bringing with it some guilt that she had ever allowed herself to become pregnant. Yet how she so wanted that baby, imagined herself holding it, loving it…a love child.

In the kitchen again, she sat at the table, her head in her hands. Nausea, partly as a result of the sickness of early pregnancy and partly from the shock of the verbal attack, swept over her so that she fought to keep down the contents of her stomach. She was puzzled by the oddity of it all. Rafe would marry one day— how could they stop him? Perhaps they had an agenda, the step-family, in which she did not figure, or a marriage for Rafe in the near future. After all, he did not have a relationship with them.

As the minutes ticked by and she breathed deeply,

she gradually came to the realization that she would not tell Rafe. She was deeply frightened, not sure why. No, she would not tell him…not yet, perhaps not at all. She opened her eyes and stared unseeingly ahead. Yes, that would be best, because she could not imagine the scene where she would tell him, or what good could come out of it.

That decision came to her as her mind ranged quickly over the recent scene where she had told Rafe about the pregnancy when they had been living together for about six months. The revelation had not been planned quite that way, it had just happened inadvertently. Winter had been giving way to a cool spring when she had realized she was pregnant. Two days of vomiting in the early morning had warned her. It had happened on days when she had been off duty, and Rafe had already left for work. Others signs had also been present, which she had confirmed by taking a pregnancy test.

A sense of joy had been tempered by her concern that Rafe would think she had trapped him. They had been carried away, careless in their happiness.

It was after a weekend of Rafe being on call that she told him. He had been working solidly for twenty-four hours without a break, all the Sunday night, and came home early on the Monday morning while Lilly was preparing to go to work. Almost ready to leave, she found herself overcome by a wave of nausea and went quickly to lean over the toilet in the main bathroom.

"Lilly, are you sick?" Rafe's voice from the open doorway made her jump, not having heard him come into the house. Lilly straightened up to look at him, shocked by how exhausted and pale he looked, as pale as she must look herself. Beads of sweat edged her face and she felt cold.

She had hoped it would not be like this, the telling: she had wanted to pick the time and place. It was all wrong.

Struck anew by how attractive he was, how much she loved and needed him, she stared back at him, momentarily at a loss. He was a tall, well-built, attractive man in an understated way that she found very appealing. His hair, cut fairly short, was a dark blond, with a slight wave to it as it stood up thickly from his high, broad forehead. He had a straight nose, a lean, angular face and a very masculine mouth. His eyes were an unusual dark grey colour, not quite blue.

"I...didn't hear you come in," she said, swallowing saliva and the feeling of sickness. "Yes, I am feeling a little sick."

When he came into the bathroom, his eyes on her face, she could tell that he had a very good idea of why she was feeling sick. For a long moment they stood and looked at each other while she fought the urge to vomit up the small amount of weak tea and the piece of dry toast that she had had for her breakfast.

"Are you pregnant?" he asked quietly, matter-of-factly, with no particular inflection in his voice. That matter-of-factness sent a chill through her. She had thought he would take her into his arms, twirl her around with joy…or something like that. Then she reminded herself that she was living in real life, not in a fairy-tale.

"Yes," she said, swallowing convulsively. "I…I've known for sure for about a week." Then, because his stunned expression did not change, because his face was so haggard with tiredness, she added in a whisper, "I'm sorry." Fear began to flutter in her chest, like soft fingers playing on her heart, which she recognized instinctively as the fear of rejection.

He closed his eyes, put a hand up to press his fingers against his closed lids. "It's been a horrendous night," he said slowly. "Forgive me if I don't react in a way you might expect. I can't seem to take this in. There was a bad accident on the highway involving five vehicles. Several of the patients we worked on are in the intensive care unit on life support, at least one not expected to make it. There were several kids… Thank God I didn't have to deal with them. I'm still there mentally… Sorry."

"You must be ready to drop," she said, forcing a normalcy to her voice that she was far from feeling.

"There's some tea made in the kitchen." As a trauma nurse herself in the surgical unit of the operating suite at the hospital, she could visualize the scene only too well.

"Thanks. Are you all right?" Only then did he move forward and put his arms round her, holding her against his body. "Sorry you've been here all alone, feeling rotten," he said. "Why didn't you tell me sooner?"

"Well, I wanted to choose the moment," Lilly said ruefully, forcing a lightness to her voice. "Instead, I seem to have had it chosen for me." It was only because she had wanted to set the scene that this felt all wrong. His exhaustion and her sickness were the dominant aspects.

Uppermost in her mind and her observations was what Rafe didn't do. Although he had his arms around her, he didn't kiss her, stroke her hair and tell her that he was happy that she was pregnant. Instead, he drew back a little and looked at her with serious, tired eyes.

"Well, I don't know exactly what to say," he said. "I would like to have children at some point. I'm not sure if now is the right time. Saying that doesn't help you right now, I know."

"Sorry," she whispered, determined not to let him see her confusion and the tears that threatened to form in her eyes. Perhaps he meant that he didn't want to have children with her. Somehow she couldn't bring herself to ask.

"It's not your fault," he said, pulling her against him once more. "I should have been more careful. Maybe you should stay at home today to rest."

It sounded to her that he was, perhaps, making the assumption that she didn't want a baby right now. "Oh, no," she said quickly. "If I'd done that, I would have taken the week off, and I want to go to work."

"What are we to do?" he asked her, standing back from her, holding her at arm's length. "I'll be in a better position to think about it later. I can't think straight right now. We'll talk when you get home. Right?"

"Yes," she agreed, working hard to make that word sound normal when she wanted to sob. Maybe she was too sensitive, imputing motives to him that he did not have. "I...I want this baby, Rafe. That's not in question."

"Right," he said. Then he did kiss her gently on the mouth. "Sorry I'm so distracted. There are a lot of images in my mind which are going to haunt me for some time, to join all the others I have there."

Lilly nodded her understanding. "I can imagine." After all, her news was not the only thing in the world. Life went on.

What she had discovered was that his calm competence and confidence in the operating room masked a strong compassion and empathy for his patients, which inevitably took a toll on him, in spite of his techniques—ones that they all had—for distancing himself. You distanced yourself by knowing that you did what you could professionally, to the best of your ability, and that if a patient died there had been nothing more that could have been done by anyone.

"We'll talk about it later," she confirmed, barely able to get the words out because her lips felt stiff. Had she expected him to be overjoyed?

"Should we get married, do you think?" he said.

"Oh, no." The words came out quickly as she was startled by the casualness of it, thinking that he could not be serious. "I don't think it's ever a good idea to marry because of a pregnancy. There…there have to be other reasons, too. I…I don't want you to feel trapped, or whatever. This wasn't something I planned." As she said the words, she knew that she believed them. There had to be other compelling reasons to marry. It had to be right in the first place, for both of them. For her it was right, but she was not sure about him.

"I didn't think it was something you planned," he said. "I wouldn't feel trapped. It's just not the optimum time, that's all. Maybe there never is an optimum time."

Because he seemed dazed with shock, Lilly leaned forward and kissed him on the cheek. "See you later today," she said. "Get some sleep." Then she picked up her bag and rain jacket and headed for the door.

"Wait!" he said, striding after her. When he took

her into his arms again she stiffened. "I love you, Lilly. You take care. We'll talk tonight."

"Yes," she whispered. "Love you, too."

She left the house to walk the short distance to the subway station and the train that would take her to within a very short walking distance of the hospital where she worked.

Only when she was off her street did she let the tears that she had been holding back trickle down her cheeks. There was no one to see. At this time of early morning there were very few people about, only one or two walking their dogs in the quiet residential area before going to work themselves. There had been a feeling that this time in her life would somehow be momentous, when she told the father of her child she was pregnant.

By the time she got to the subway station she had composed herself.

Now, sitting at the kitchen table in the home they shared, she mulled over all this. There was no doubt, she thought, that the hormone changes of pregnancy made one's emotions more labile. Yet there was more to it than that. Former insecurities from childhood were coming back to haunt her overwhelmingly. Yes, they had talked things over, had decided to leave things as they were for now. He had spoken a little about his parents' divorce, how it had affected him so that he was unsure of relationships in his own life. All he had known then, he said, was that he loved her.

To be loved by him was more than she had dared to hope for initially. When she had first met Dr Rafe Neilson, a new trauma surgeon in the operating rooms of the hospital where she worked, she had known instinctively that she was in danger of falling in love with the type of man she generally avoided, a self-confident, successful, attractive man, the type who could—at least in theory—have any woman he wanted. He was a man who could break her heart. Clearly, she could see now, she had been somewhat in awe of him. His gentleness had broken the barrier of her insecurity.

At home in her small, cosy apartment in the evening of the first day of meeting him she had written in her diary: ''Worked with a new surgeon today on a bad trauma case that came in by helicopter. Very good surgeon. We got along very well, worked well together. We shall be working together a lot. He seems very nice.'' That didn't say the half of it.

There was no way she could tell him now. Let it be.

A week after the visit of the two women, Lilly started to bleed and knew she was having a miscarriage.

The strain of keeping silent had taken its toll on her, so that when the bleeding started it seemed like a manifestation of her mental angst. Although Rafe was with her and took her to the hospital, the process continued to its inevitable conclusion.

By that point she knew that she was frightened to speak to him about his family in case there was some truth to the threat that he would be cut off from the family money because of her. Intellectually, she didn't believe it, while emotionally she felt now that it was possible.

When she arrived home from the hospital, she told him that she had to leave. It seemed to her that someone else was talking for her, saying something that was nonetheless inevitable.

"I must go," she said. "I...need to be on my own for a while."

"Why?" he asked. "I want you with me. I want to help you."

"I don't really know why...except that I must get away for a while to think," she said. "I want to stay with my parents in Albertstown for a while."

His tense stillness told her that he had expected something of the sort.

"I love you," she told Rafe sadly, "but I have to get myself sorted out."

"Can't you do that here with me?" he asked tersely.

"I don't think I can."

"I don't know how I'll function without you," he said. "Come back to me when you're ready. Will you?"

"Perhaps…" she said. How could she tell that he really meant it?

"Don't cut me off, Lilly," he said. "Stay in touch, talk to me, otherwise I'm going to go crazy."

"I won't cut you off," she said, while secretly feeling the future to be a blank. "Just give me some time."

"What will you do?"

"Maybe I'll leave the city for a while. I don't want to blame you in any way, but if you had reacted differently to the news that I was pregnant that time I first told you, perhaps things would have been different. Perhaps…perhaps I'm being over-sensitive, but I interpreted that as rejection, of me and the child."

There was a loaded silence, in which she sensed that he was weighing his words, that he had a lot to say to her but decided not to say it. "I think you're depressed, Lilly," he said. "Clinically depressed."

Lilly shrugged. "Yes, I expect I am depressed," she said.

He pulled her against him and held her tight. "I wanted that baby, too," he said softly. "You have to believe that."

"I don't know what I believe," she said.

Lilly had the odd feeling that she was standing outside herself, watching herself, while inside she was crying. All she knew was that she needed to get away from him for a while to give herself a chance to sort herself out and him a chance to decide about her. Her love for him, her attraction to him, blotted out everything else, and she had to behave sensibly. If he really wanted her, he would eventually come after her…she believed that. Fate would decide.

They talked into the night, lying side by side, their hands touching. Lilly found that her grief at the loss of the baby blotted out everything else. When Rafe held her in his arms and said, "I love you. We'll have other babies," she found that she could not believe him.

Try as she might to tell him about the visit from his step-family, the words would not come. After a while that silence was like a barrier between them, a barrier that only she could see in her mind's eye.

She lay there, thinking about her work at the hospital, where she seemed to function normally. Outside work she had begun to wonder whether she was having a nervous breakdown, the past combining with the present to force her to confront unfinished business. At odd moments when she was alone, she felt tears dripping slowly down her cheeks. The sense of humour that had always stood her in good stead in times of crisis had gone.

The love she felt for that baby mingled with her sense of mourning. Now she understood that you only mourned that which you loved. Grief is the price you have to pay for love, she had read somewhere. It was odd that love did not go away when its object was no longer there—that was why it was so difficult to bear.

With Rafe, whom she also loved, she had to give him a chance to get away from her, she had to test him. If he did not come after her, so be it.

As she lay sleepless beside Rafe, listening to his even breathing, she began tentatively to think that she might contact the medical and nursing organization World Aid to find work and leave her job at University Hospital, or take leave of absence to move back into her parents' house away from the city.

## CHAPTER TWO

THE passengers in the plane could see smoke quite a long way before their destination, the small logging town of Crater Lake in northern Ontario, Canada. Sitting by a window, Lilly looked out, taking in the scene as far as she could see in all directions.

The plane flew relatively low over densely wooded areas of conifers and deciduous trees as they came to the northern areas of the province. From her vantage point the smoke looked initially like a fine mist. There were thousands of acres of forest so fires in them would be a major disaster. She had found herself a job with World Aid and this was where she had been sent to on her initial assignment, together with another nurse from the organization. Rafe and Toronto, her family, all suddenly seemed very far away.

As the plane droned steadily north, showing them the first view of smoke, the enormity of what they were about to confront gradually and soberly impressed itself on Lilly.

"Welcome to reality, kid." She said the words to herself, looking through the window at the dense carpet of green beneath them. The power of nature was asserting its own reality. A human being, down in that, would be pretty puny, even at the best of times.

"We don't want any do-gooders," the recruiter at the World Aid headquarters in Toronto had told her bluntly, "because, in our experience, do-gooders turn and run when there is real, desperate need—and we are dealing with real, desperate need. Also, we don't want anyone who has a "significant other" to leave behind, or anyone who is running away from something. Do those things applying to you, Ms Page?"

"No," she had said, wondering if she was lying through her teeth, as the old saying went. Then she knew that her sense of humour was creeping back, something that she would need, no doubt, in the isolated and threatened community of Crater Lake. Nonetheless, the ache in her heart was ever-present.

As they got closer to Crater Lake, they saw denser smoke that hung in the air like clouds. No mistaking now that it was smoke. Lilly exchanged meaningful glances with the nurse, Ashley Soper, who sat beside her, whom she had met at an orientation session at the World Aid headquarters. "Welcome to Crater Lake," Ashley said soberly.

When the plane landed on a bumpy air strip at Crater Lake, there was no mistaking the smoke. As soon as the plane door was opened they could smell it. No one on the plane said much as they shuffled with their carry-on bags to the metal steps that had been wheeled up to the aircraft door. Most of the people on the flight had come to deal with the fires in one way or another.

The other thing that assaulted their senses was the heat and the humidity. It was the month of June now, a particularly hot June, which had not brought any rain. There was a severe drought here in Crater Lake.

As Lilly walked down the steps, looking around her at the very rural setting and the tiny airstrip, with its scattering of small buildings, she felt something of an impostor. What did she know about fires? She only saw the very end result in her high-tech hospital in the heart of the city. Well, she told herself, she would soon find out. To her credit, she had done some quick preliminary reading about forest fires in the brief time that she had had between knowing of her assignment and taking off, which had informed her that most forest fires were started by dry lightning—lightning with no rain.

Various people were waiting in the small building, holding signs identifying themselves, as the passengers straggled in from the tarmac.

"Someone is supposed to meet us here," Ashley said, a few paces ahead of Lilly. "I was told that they don't know our names but will just have a sign saying WORLD AID."

"Right," Lilly said, scanning the small crowd of waiting people who were milling about.

"There it is!" Ashley said, after a few moments. "I can see a guy holding a sign. That's us, Lilly. Over there by that exit." She pointed. "Come on."

Lilly followed her a few paces, then looked ahead

to where Ashley had pointed. Then she stopped, rooted to the spot, and dropped her bag at her feet, feeling the blood draining from her face. Ashley went on ahead of her.

Surely, it couldn't be? A feeling of intense unreality—brought on by the smell of smoke, the unfamiliar surroundings and the man she was looking at—came over her, so that she could not take a step forward. Quite suddenly she felt faint and sick. Ashley stopped and looked back at her curiously.

The tall man standing near an exit, holding the cardboard sign was Rafe Neilson. His hair had been cut very short, and he was wearing army fatigues.

"Oh, my God," she whispered. "What is he doing here?" The question, incredulously, answered itself. Since he was holding the sign, he was obviously with World Aid. Bewildered, she could not take it in.

Instinctively, she looked behind her at the way they had come, her eyes searching for the glass doors and the aircraft beyond, desperately wanting an escape route. There was no way out, nowhere to hide. Paradoxically, she yearned for him at the same time that she needed to be away from him; she wanted to escape at the same time that she wanted to run to him, to tell him that she had missed him. The tall, masculine figure in the unfamiliar clothing did not seem to belong to her any more. He was an enigmatic stranger. Had she really lain in his arms and been pregnant with his child?

As she turned back and looked at him, he also saw her and started to walk towards her, his eyes fixed on her face. Even from that distance she could tell that he was as shocked to see her as she was to see him. Trying to cover up, Lilly picked up her bag and went forward, concentrating on putting one foot in front of the other.

His face was pale and he looked exhausted, as he had often looked when they had lived together, as well as considerably thinner than when she had seen him last. He walked straight past Ashley and came up to her, stood looking down at her, his eyes blazing with a look of absolute incredulity.

"Lilly," he said. "What the hell are you doing here?" His voice sounded cracked with fatigue.

"I…um…" she floundered. "I…could ask you the same." Although she knew, of course, as he was holding the sign, down by his side now. "World Aid sent me here."

"This is no place for you," he said, his eyes blazing down into hers. "Are you mad? This place could go up in flames any day now."

"You mean it's all right for you to put your life on the line, but not me?" she countered.

Instinctively she wanted to go into his arms, to be held by him, as she would have been in the near past. In the past weeks he had never been out of her mind; now it was amazingly wonderful to see him in the flesh, although she didn't know what to do about it.

"Yes, I do mean that," he said. "When I last saw you, you were pretty vulnerable."

"I'll manage," she said, staring back at him challengingly.

They looked at each other for long moments while Ashley, seeing that they obviously knew each other, stayed back at a respectable distance.

"I'm with a colleague," she added.

Rafe let out a long sigh. Then, oddly, they both made an instinctive move towards each other, as though to embrace and kiss. Lilly felt herself swaying forward towards him, even as her eyes went over his face, taking in every familiar feature that she loved so much. He seemed to have aged somewhat, mainly from exhaustion, she suspected.

Then they both stiffened as though they remembered simultaneously that they no longer belonged together.

"A-and you?" she stammered.

"Yes, as you see. I'm surprised they would send you here on your first assignment," he said. "I've taken leave of absence for a month, I needed to get away. The last thing I needed was to meet up with you." He added the last sentence bitterly, so that Lilly stared at him in open-mouthed shock.

"What do you mean?" she whispered. People were milling around them and they were oblivious.

"I don't need to have to deal with you in this place," he said, staring at her grimly. "This place is serious business. Haven't you done enough to wreck my life?''

"What?''

"You heard me,'' he said, his face and voice taut as he looked down at her with narrowed eyes. "I don't suppose you thought of it from my angle, did you? Since you've been gone, I've had time to think. I can't see that I did anything to you to make you up and leave, or to come up to a place like this. On the contrary, I thought I did what I possibly could to support you.''

"I…I'm with a colleague,'' she repeated, seeing Ashley coming back.

At that moment, Ashley came up to them. "Um… excuse me,'' she said. "Are you the person who is meeting us?''

"Yes,'' Rafe said turning round to her, extending a hand. "Sorry. It's just that Lilly and I…know each other, you might say. I'm Rafe Neilson, MD, formerly of University Hospital. Pleased to meet you.''

"Ashley Soper. Pleased to meet you, too,'' Ashley said, politely containing her curiosity about him and Lilly. "Have you been up here long?''

"This is my first assignment,'' he said. "I've been up here for four days, working with the army medics. We're certainly needed.''

"I wasn't expecting to smell smoke as soon as we got off the aircraft,'' Ashley said.

"You can't get away from it,'' he said. "A lot of

the people who live up here have been evacuated, as well as a lot of those who're working up here temporarily. It's like a war zone. It's not all burns, there are lots of other injuries and heat exhaustion. Some of the fires are not that far from the edge of town. There are teams fighting to save the buildings, keeping them hosed down with water.''

Scarcely taking in what he was saying, Lilly listened in a daze. His ambivalence about seeing her matched her own.

''I'm to drive you to the camp,'' he said, looking from her to Ashley. ''We're set up on the edge of town in the grounds of a recreation centre so that we can use their facilities and their parking lot. That serves as a helicopter pad. It's all temporary. It's the only suitable place, even though it's at the end of town closest to the fires.''

''This may be a stupid question,'' Ashley said, ''but is it safe?''

''I don't think anywhere's safe around here,'' he said. ''We have to be prepared to move quickly if the wind shifts and the fire gets too close. There are always planes on the ground here, in case we have to evacuate in a hurry. We may not get more than a few minutes' notice.''

There were so many questions she wanted to ask Rafe…like why he had taken leave of absence. There was a tension and anger in him that was almost palpable, evidently obvious to her nursing colleague.

Emotions churned inside her and she didn't know what to say. Looking at him now, she knew that she could never be indifferent to him. Lesson number one, learnt at Crater Lake, she thought ruefully.

"Over here to pick up your bags," Rafe said, indicating a small conveyor belt. "It takes them a while to unload here, so we just have to be patient."

Scarcely noticing where she was going or what was going on around her, Lilly followed him. The question "Are you running away from anyone or anything?" repeated itself now in her brain. Perhaps, after all, she had told a lie about that. Paradoxically, she had wanted to get away from Rafe, yet had wanted to be with him at the same time. Now she had literally run almost into his arms in this remote place.

"I would probably have requested another posting had I known you were coming here," Rafe said to her quietly, as they stood side by side. "The last thing they want is two people who have had a relationship that has gone wrong." The bitterness in his voice was something new to her. Perhaps she hadn't given much thought to the possibility that she might have hurt him. He had always seemed so confident, competent...

Lesson number two?

As they waited for their luggage, Lilly stood by numbly. Ashley had no inhibitions and asked Rafe all sorts of questions. Lilly felt hysterical laughter bubbling up inside her, while she was close to tears at the same time. If he said a wrong word she would howl.

It would be great if she could have a good laugh, she thought cynically.

It was pretty amusing, in a peculiar sort of way, that the man she had been trying to avoid whenever she went to Toronto, putting on dark glasses in the street, for instance, had been waiting for her in this remote place. There was something almost slapstick about it. Crater Lake wasn't the most romantic place in the world, and never would be. Even though they were surrounded by some fantastic wild country, there would be no time to enjoy it. They were there to work.

While Ashley and Rafe talked about the fires and the set-up that awaited them, Lilly remained mostly silent, watching grimly for their bags to appear. Tiredness and hunger were beginning to kick in now, and those made one vulnerable to mood swings and poor judgement, she knew that from experience. That was even more likely to happen in the field—they had been told that at World Aid.

Eventually, they were installed in an army jeep, the two of them sitting behind Rafe, their bags stowed in the back. Lilly felt overawed and disorientated, looking at the back of Rafe's shorn head, wanting to reach forward to stroke it.

The road from the airstrip to the community wound through dense forest. The smell of smoke was unmistakable as they proceeded, and as they came into the main street of the town she could see little bits of ash floating about in the air like snowflakes.

"It's not far." Rafe said, raising his voice above the sound of the engine. "Nothing's very far in this place. Memorize the route, so that if we have to get out fast and you have to make it to the airport on foot, you know which way to go."

Lilly looked at Ashley, feeling the first twinges of fear mixed with the anticipation of being about to do some useful work. It was all overlaid with the sense of severe unreality at being in the company of Rafe. Get over it, she told herself sternly. Pull yourself together. This was no place in which to be self-indulgent about one's personal life. She was there to do a specific job to the best of her ability, and she was going to do it.

As they drove into the enormous parking lot of the recreation centre it was obvious that the army had taken it over, with tents large and small in every available space, with a little left over for parking. There was one very large, single-storey building and some smaller hut-like buildings around it. All around the edges of the parking area was a wide grassy verge on which more army tents had been pitched. Beyond that was dense forest.

Lilly and Ashley took all this in as Rafe swung the Jeep off the main road, which had come through the centre of the small community of Crater Lake, onto the paved area and parked near the tents.

"This is where you'll sleep," Rafe said, getting out of the jeep, unfolding his long legs in a quick economical movement, indicating a specific tent. "At least, for now."

While they were sluggishly getting themselves out of the unfamiliar Jeep, which was rather high off the ground, Rafe had already unloaded their bags and was carrying them into the tent. As Lilly approached the tent, she could see that the outside of it was covered with a fine black dust, which she identified as soot.

Inside, there were four basic camp beds set up, with only one looking as though it had an owner, with a rucksack and an army jacket on top of it. There was mosquito netting hanging down from a contraption in the roof of the tent, one for each bed.

"Dump your stuff," Rafe instructed, "then report at the recreation centre. Someone there will tell you what to do, and you'll get a meal. I'll see you later."

With that, he turned on his heel and marched out, as though he couldn't wait to get away from her, Lilly thought. With his very short hair and alien clothing, he seemed almost like a stranger to her. Certainly she was looking at him with new eyes, all her good intentions to stay away from him in tatters, so that she could scarcely remember what they were. Not to see him again, as a possibility, had been one of them. Now she seemed to have entered a new world where everything, including herself, had been changed. Feeling stunned, she watched him go.

"Thanks," Ashley called after him. "He seems like a really nice guy, if a little brusque," she added, when he was out of earshot. "So you two know each other! Pretty well, I get the impression… Hmm?"

"Yes. I'll tell you about it some time, Ashley," Lilly said wearily, knowing that had she been on her own she would probably let go and howl. "If there's ever a spare moment here. I'm having my doubts. He was the last person I expected to see here. I'd no idea he was with World Aid."

"You'll sure get your priorities sorted out in a place like this," Ashley said.

"Yeah. The first thing I'm going to do is go to the loo and have a quick wash of face and hands. Then I'm going to have the biggest plate of nosh I've ever had. We're going to need that," Lilly said, trying to add lightness to her tone, while she felt a sense of dissonance that made her feel that she was losing a grip on her sanity. "With lots of salt," she added firmly.

"Right!" Ashley agreed. "I'm sweating like a horse."

As they were about to leave, a young woman soldier came in, dressed in fatigues and heavy, dusty leather boots. It was obvious that she had been in the fire zone. Her face was sooty and her bedraggled hair, which had been scraped back into a ponytail and held with an elastic band, was bursting its bond. Her eyes were bloodshot and glazed with fatigue.

"Hi, I'm Corporal Jessie Kemp," she said, holding out a grimy hand. "Just come to get a bit of shut-eye.'' She went to her camp bed, threw the rucksack and jacket on the floor, unfolded a slim bed roll to make a mattress, then sat down and began to unlace her boots. ''I won't disturb you guys. I work mainly at night—all hours, really—fire-watching on the ground and putting out root fires. There's a lot of digging, and stuff. Bloody hard work.''

Quickly she eased her feet out of the boots, pulled off her socks while she was talking, took off her outer camouflage shirt to reveal a sweat-soaked T-shirt, and swung her legs up onto the bed with a long, drawn-out, ''A-a-a-h!'' Her eyes closed and her features slackened.

Lilly and Ashley crept around silently, arranging their stuff, then set a brisk pace over to the main building. On the way they passed a shower hut, which had a sign outside. The main building had showers inside, separate ones for men and women, off a corridor, then in the main area there was a kitchen with a serving hatch, and tables and chairs in a dining area.

A sergeant sat at a reception table inside the vast hall. ''Hi, ladies,'' he said, eyeing them astutely. ''You'll be with World Aid, right? The two nurses.''

''Yes,'' Lilly said, feeling a little as though she were back at school. ''I'm Lilly Page and this is Ashley Soper.''

''Good.'' He ticked something off on a clipboard. ''Ask for something to eat here. They always have some food on the go. Get yourselves a couple of bottles of water each and remember to drink a lot and take salt with your food. You sweat a lot here and you don't want to get dehydrated. We have to do everything we can not to become a liability to our colleagues. Ms Soper, you'll work in the medic tent number two, with the army doc, who happens to be on duty right now. Ms. Page you'll work in medic tent one with Dr Neilson, also from World Aid. The docs will orientate you to what you have to do. Thank you for coming here, ladies, and good luck.'' Although he didn't add ''You're going to need it'', his expression said it all as he allowed himself a slight grin in dismissing them.

Lilly had been about to open her mouth to protest that she didn't want to work with Rafe Neilson, but then thought better of it. The last thing they needed here were prima donnas who started to complain about the conditions before they had done a hand's turn of work, as her dad would have put it. ''Thank you…sir,'' she said meekly, feeling intimidated by his uniform, wondering whether she should salute.

''You'll need some fatigues and some scrubsuits and fire boots,'' he said, pointing to a service hatch. ''Report there after you've eaten. They'll take a mug shot and give you an ID badge, which you'll wear at all times.''

''Right…'' Ashley said. ''Thank you.''

Lilly and Ashley backed away, then marched smartly to the other serving hatch for food.

The smell of smoke had permeated into here also, Lilly noted. Although no one around them seemed alarmed, she sensed a heightened alertness in the atmosphere and felt herself take it on also, with a sense of fear added.

The sergeant came over to them while they were eating. "Don't go off the property, ladies," he said. "We all have to be accounted for by the fire chief, and you are accountable to the army and to Dr Neilson, who's representing World Aid here. We all have to sign in and out. There's a siren if we have to evacuate, and there's a protocol for that, which you'll find out when you get to the first-aid tents. We muster here first, then at the airstrip, finally. That protocol is also posted in your tent, in all the public buildings as well, and even in the showers."

"Thanks," they mumbled, mouths full of food.

Later, in the bathroom, they changed into light-weight summer fatigues.

The medic tents were huge, dark green canvas, with red crosses on the sides and roofs.

"See you later, Lilly," Ashley said as she branched off in the parking area to go to tent number two, "and good luck."

"Thanks, I sure need it," Lilly said. "Same to you." Never in her life had she felt so disorientated and unsure of herself. It all seemed like a dream.

The interior of the tent, soothingly green, was cooled by electric fans. Almost immediately she saw

Rafe, in what she took to be a patient reception area near the entrance. At the sight of him, her heart gave that peculiar leap of recognition. She knew then that she loved him, and most likely always would. If only she could have felt right for him…

"Hi," he said, seeing her. "Come in. I'll be finished here in a few minutes, then I'll orientate you to the place and the procedures."

"All right. Thank you," she said, going into the reception area and standing to one side so that she could observe what was going on without getting in the way. An army doctor was there also, and an army medic named John. Another soldier, whom she took to be another orderly, was busily getting supplies from another small enclosed area next to the one she was in.

Rafe, she could see, was putting the finishing touches to a neck dressing on a firefighter who still had most of his protective clothing on. His face and hands were black with soot.

"Come outside," Rafe said to her quietly, when he had finished the dressing, washed his hands and had the man transferred to a rest area. "I want to talk to you."

They went outside again and moved a little away from the tent so that their voices would not carry to the men who were trying to rest inside. Once again, Lilly felt as though she were moving in a dream. From above them they could hear the drone of aircraft and the chop-chop of helicopters. Some of the planes would be water bombers, she knew, scooping up water from the lake and dropping it on the fires, as would some of the helicopters, while others would be on reconnaissance duty, fire-spotting.

"Which direction is the fire?" Lilly asked, desperate for something to say to this man who was dear and familiar, yet like a grim stranger at the same time.

"There are several fires," he said. "Some on the other side of Crater Lake." He pointed to an area opposite the recreation centre, where the lake bordered the main road that came through the centre of the town from the airstrip. "And there are some up this way, at the end of this road. The road comes to an end not far away, then all you have is forest. A lot of that is burning right now."

A thrill of fear added to Lilly's churning emotions as she stood next to the man who had been at the centre of her universe, ill at ease, not sure what to do or say next. The desire to go into his arms was overwhelming. As she looked at him now, she again registered the fatigue that appeared on his face, his eyes bloodshot, the way he looked at the hospital when he had not slept for thirty-six hours. That all seemed like another world.

"I—I find it incredible that you should be here," Lilly blurted out, stopping between two tents, turning to him. They were in relative privacy. "What about your job at the hospital? I mean…your career?"

"What about your career?" he countered, his features stiff as he looked down at her, giving her a sharp insight that while they had lived together he had been adept at hiding emotion. Perhaps he had done that to protect her. Certainly, towards the end, the focus of their dialogue had been on her.

"I—I can take a break and pick up my career again more easily," she said. "This experience should be an asset to me."

"I don't think I can work with you here," he said brusquely. "There's no way. Tomorrow I'll call World Aid and find out if there's another place they can assign you to."

"What?" she said, frowning up at him. "You just have to work with me, because I don't want to go anywhere else. This is good for a training place. What are you doing here, Rafe?"

"I needed to take some time off," he said abruptly, staring down at her as they stood rather awkwardly together. "Getting back to basics like this helps, although, God knows, I see enough life-and-death situations in the hospital. What I don't need is to have you here."

"Thanks very much for those encouraging words," she said, with uncharacteristic sarcasm and bitterness, a catch in her voice, to which he did not react. "I wasn't expecting to see you, either. But now that we're here, we just have to make the best of it."

"Do we? I don't want anyone to know about our

former relationship,'' he said. ''We're here to do a job. That's it.''

''Agreed,'' she said.

''I'm still going to make that call.''

Lilly decided not to argue now. Was it because of her that he had got out of the city? Because of what had happened between them? Lilly felt the familiar stab of guilt and sadness, like mourning.

''Is it because of us that you're here?'' she asked.

''That had something to do with it,'' he agreed.

''I'm sorry,'' she said.

''Are you?'' he said harshly. Quickly he reached forward and gripped her shoulders and pulled her against him. ''I've missed you like hell.'' He kissed her fiercely, holding her to him, enfolding her in his arms. At the touch of his mouth on hers, a wave of intense awareness engulfed her and she swayed weakly against his hard body.

Instinctively she put her arms up around his neck, responding to his kiss. Over the past lonely weeks she had dreamed of this, yet had never imagined this setting, the two of them surrounded by smoky air, large first-aid tents and an almost tangible sense of terrible fear in the atmosphere.

Just as abruptly, he let her go, so that she staggered back. ''Have you any idea what all that did to me?'' he demanded tensely, keeping his voice low. ''You wanting to leave, with little explanation? I wanted that baby, too. Because you were so upset, I didn't push my point of view. We could have worked something out, if you hadn't just got out as fast as you could. Now I think it's too late.''

It was almost a year, in the summer, since she had first met Rafe, and it had been before Christmas that they had decided to live together, going into it with a sense that they would be together for the long term. They hadn't thought it out very clearly. In those very first days and then weeks of knowing each other, they had gravitated towards each other as though the link had been preordained. It had been an odd feeling, somewhat awe-inspiring to Lilly, as she'd felt that she'd had no control over it, that she was being swept along by events that had already been decided somehow by fate, or whatever one wanted to call it.

''I know you were the one who went through the miscarriage,'' he said, ''but did you think about how I felt?''

Lilly ran a hand distractedly through her short, dark hair, which was becoming plastered to her scalp with sweat. ''I don't know,'' she said, feeling very close to tears and out of control. ''Perhaps I didn't…not enough, anyway. I wanted to get away, to have time to think. The miscarriage had the effect of…bringing me abruptly back to…to what I felt at the time was reality.''

''Reality for whom?'' he said harshly.

''For me,'' she said. ''We…we were living in a sort of dream world. It was great while it lasted.''

"I didn't think it was a dream world," he said. "To me, that was about as real as it gets—living with a woman, loving her, having a child."

"I don't belong in your world, Rafe, because I don't understand it. Of course I've missed you…so much. Now here you are. It's—it's bizarre. I don't know what to think, or do." Her voice wobbled with emotion and tears pricked her eyes.

They stood looking at each other, each waiting for the other to break the impasse. The attraction between them, which had always been strong, held her once more in its grip, so that she felt pulled towards him by invisible forces that she did not understand. If only she could take him at face value, accept what he had to offer.

It was difficult to tell a man that you could not accept him because you feared future rejection, because you thought he might grow tired of you, because you thought maybe you were not good enough for him, whatever that really meant. Then there was the idea that he would already know all that anyway, could sense it, see it, be aware of it in all they did together. All she knew was that the pain and confusion were very real and powerful, so much so that they had taken over her life. The verbal attacks by his step-family had confirmed what she had feared all along, she could see that now.

So much of it was irrational, she recognized that. Before Rafe, she had often chosen men who were flawed in some way, because she felt that she could not cope with super-confident men, lovely, well-rounded men like Rafe…although her father was that way. Yet, before long, those other men had bored and frustrated her because of their inadequacies. All that was apparent to her as she stood looking at the man she still loved, still wanted, but with whom she did not know how to find a way out.

"And how do you see my world?" he asked.

"You…you've had a sheltered and privileged youth, in spite of the divorce…most of what you could ever want…money…the sort of security that I never knew existed." Her voice trailed off. "We've said all this before, in other words."

"Don't you believe it," he said, with a new bitterness. "As much as I still like my father, most of the time, mainly because he is my father, I have no illusions about him. He liked to control everything and everyone within his orbit. That's why my mother left. He did it with money, giving it or not giving it as he saw fit. Money is a great manipulator. He did it with affection, too, giving or withholding. He did it with time and attention. What kids need is affection, attention and time, as well as basic protection. He got away with his inadequacies most of the time because he had a certain charm to go with it."

"I didn't know," Lilly said despairingly.

"I didn't want to bore you, talking about him, because really he doesn't figure a great deal in my life any more," he said forcefully. "I can take him or leave him, thank God. At the same time, I can't pretend that all that hasn't affected me...my ability to make relationships, to trust."

"Yes, I can see that it would," she said. "It's odd that we would have to come all the way up here for you to say that."

"This is an odd situation," he said. "My mother once said that he liked to do her thinking for her, and she had to get out in order to get her mind back. She got sick of being manipulated. I earn my own living, I don't ask anyone for anything...except that my love be returned, my loyalty."

"You...you came here because of me?" she said wonderingly. "Because of us?"

"Yes," he said. "So maybe you can see that I don't think I want to work with you, Lilly. You wanted out of my life. So be it. Been there, done that."

"Well, I..." She took a step back from him, looking around frantically like a cornered animal looking for a way of escape.

"This was to have been a cathartic experience for me," he said, "after which I could, maybe, get on with my life. I wanted you out of my system—and now here you are."

"I...I suggest that we start work. We're here to work," she said.

"Don't tell me that we're here to work," he said with an edge of sarcasm that was out of character.

"That will sort itself out, one way or the other." She swallowed nervously, the desire to weep very close to the surface. "Or not."

"Or not just about sums it up," he said. "I want you the hell out of here."

"Let's not hurt each other, Rafe," she said sadly. "Please. There's been enough of that already. It has mostly to do with me. I'm very mixed up."

Rafe stared at her tensely, as though he would say more, then he simply said, "Come on. I'll show you what I know about the routine here. What I've picked up in the last four days."

As they emerged from between the two tents, there was a thin veil of smoke all around them, the smell of it in their nostrils and their throats. Little bits of ash floated by from time to time, grey or black, like snow. Silently, by mutual consent, they walked out into the centre of the parking lot to get a better view of the hills beyond the end of the road. From that direction, still quite far away, they could see a thick pall of black smoke. Presumably the firefighters were very aware of which way the wind was blowing, and that at the moment it was blowing the flames away from the community where they were. If the wind shifted, it could be a different story.

At the entrance to the tent, she touched his arm. "Please," she said quietly, "don't make that call, Rafe. I need to be here. And by the look of that fire, we may not be here more than a few days anyway."

''We'll see,'' he said grimly.

Lilly followed him into their work tent. There was so much to think about, so much to do. Although she wanted to howl and sob, there was no way she could give in to that. This was a war zone of sorts, and she was in the front line.

## CHAPTER THREE

DOING her best to disengage herself from her emotional turmoil with Rafe, Lilly followed him into the main body of the huge tent.

Here there were several soldiers lying on camp beds, as well as some civilian firefighters, while in smaller screened-off areas, near the entrance, there were treatment cubicles which contained stretchers that served as examination and treatment tables. All was bathed in a soothing green light, from the green of the canvas.

The whole place looked as though it could be dismantled and moved quickly, as indeed it might need to be, Lilly speculated as she looked around her curiously to see what equipment they had to work with and what they would have to do without. The supplies were in large plastic boxes.

"Most of our patients right now are suffering from severe fatigue, dehydration and stress," Rafe said to her quietly, very much the professional now, as though they had never met before. "A few are feeling the effects of smoke inhalation. They're resting under observation. A few have burns, not too serious. None of them wants to be airlifted out, they want to hang on with their buddies, to keep working. Which is just as well, from what I can see. Every area is short of workers.''

"What will I have to do?'' Lilly asked.

"You'll work with me,'' he said, looking at her consideringly, his casual stance of hands in pockets of his green scrub pants belied by a tension that she could sense in him. He might as well have said "until I can get you shipped out'' because it was there in the tone of his voice, but he did not say it.

"It will be our job initially to work in the reception areas of the tents, be responsible for triage,'' he went on, "then we'll be involved in the treatments and the ongoing care of those who need to rest and have intravenous fluids if they're dehydrated. We take our cues from the army doctors, as they're in charge. We have to be mindful that this is a training exercise for us, yet we have to be prepared to help with anything.''

As Rafe talked, Lilly realized more fully how much she had missed him. That they had actually lived together now seemed like part of the dream that she was living. In some ways, he seemed remote from her, and in her present state of mind she didn't know how she had dredged up the confidence to agree to live with him. He was a man who liked women, she thought now, as she had always thought, and didn't mind showing it. Yet he was certainly not what one would call a ladies' man, never that. He was the sort of man who could be loyal to one woman, the woman he loved...

"What about emergency evacuation?" Lilly asked, bringing her mind back to the job in hand, trying to dismiss her poignant sense of loss. There was so much to learn, in such a short time, if they were to be of much use. Most of all, they did not want to be a liability to those they were supposed to assist.

"There will be a siren," Rafe said, "if we have to get out. There are buses standing by at all times to take us to the airstrip. It's our responsibility to get our patients out. Keep your bags packed at all times, your personal ID with you. If you leave the camp, you must sign out and give your destination, then sign in when you return. My advice is not to leave the camp. If the siren goes, get patients onto the buses or the ambulances, then go to the tent to get your gear and get on yourself. Make sure you have been accounted for by the officer in charge of the evacuation."

"What about all the equipment?" Lilly asked.

"That will be dismantled and packed up by the soldiers," he said. "They can get these tents down pretty quickly.

"Any serious cases get airlifted out," he added.

"Right," Lilly said, forcing herself to concentrate on work. "I think I'm beginning to get the picture. All the civilians have been evacuated, so I understand?"

"All except a very few who have elected to stay

behind to fight the fire on their properties. They have to report regularly to the fire chief, who has to know where they are at all times. If he tells them to get out, they have to go.''

Lilly shivered. ''How safe are we, right here in this community centre?''

''Not safe,'' he said. ''If it were safe, we wouldn't be here.''

''No, I don't suppose we would,'' she said thoughtfully, thinking that they would be all right working together, as they always had been, if they could keep things on a professional level while they were actually on the job.

He showed her the treatment cubicles and the reception area. ''Stay with me for a couple of cases,'' he said. ''Then you can be on your own for most of the time.''

Lilly nodded. In moments, before she had time to gather her thoughts, they were confronted by two firefighters who came in together.

''Hi, how can I help you guys?'' Rafe asked, directing them into a treatment cubicle. Wordlessly, Lilly followed, prepared to stay in the background for now until she was asked to do something.

''We're both feeling pretty exhausted,'' one of the men said. ''Dizzy, nauseated. I've been drinking, but maybe it wasn't enough. We're low on salt, too, I guess.''

''Take your boots off and lie down there,'' Rafe

instructed, indicating two stretchers. "We're both volunteers with World Aid Services, attached to the army
for now. I'm Dr Rafe Neilson, and this is Lilly Page."

"Glad to meet you," they chorused. They struggled
out of their boots and outer fireproof jump suits, then
subsided wearily onto stretchers.

"Gee, it's good to lie down," one of them said.
"I've lost track of when I last had a good sleep."

"Sleep? What's that?" the other one said wearily,
closing his eyes. There was space in the area for two
stretchers, so they lay more or less side by side.

The men had brought with them the added scent of
smoke, which clung to their heavy fireproof clothing,
and it now filled the confined space.

"We take temperature, pulse rate, blood pressure—
the usual routine stuff first," Rafe said quietly to Lilly.
"You could do one, while I do the other. I like to give
them a bit of oxygen for a while, just to make sure
there's no smoke inhalation problem. Then we'll put
in intravenous lines, give normal saline initially."

Lilly nodded, not trusting her voice. It was almost
like old times, and the feeling of disorientation grew
in her. Only this seemed a new, harder Rafe, with his
new military haircut, his leanness, a seriousness that
she had not seen before. In addition, he was blaming
her, it seemed, for their break-up.

She watched him as he wheeled two small portable
oxygen tanks, coded white, to the heads of the stretchers. Each tank had a clear plastic tube and mask at-

tached to it for connecting to the patient. Quickly she moved forward to one of the tanks, adjusted a mask on the face of the man nearest to her, turned on the valve on the tank, adjusted the flow of oxygen on a flow-meter. Then she helped her patient ease an arm out of his clothing so that she could take his blood pressure. All the time she explained what she was doing. It was evident that these men had received oxygen many times before as they maintained a stoic equanimity.

"We fill in one of these treatment forms as we go along," Rafe said, handing her a sheet of printed paper, standing close so that she was tensely aware of his physical presence. What a fool she had been to think that she could forget about him eventually. That would never happen.

As Lilly worked, part of her mind was on Rafe, now so near. He was a very masculine man, yet with an empathy and gentleness that made him difficult to resist, very attractive to women. There was no arrogance in him, something that appealed to her, in sharp contrast to many of the surgeons she had worked with in her career. Because they had lived together, had shared so much, she felt that he would, in some way, always belong to her. She wondered, with a wry grin, what the people at World Aid headquarters would say if she informed them that she had met up with her erstwhile "significant other". If Rafe had his way, he would be doing just that.

"The top priority initially, after giving the oxygen," Rafe was saying to her quietly, "is to record the vital signs and to get the IV running. Most of these guys are dehydrated, some seriously. Wearing this heavy gear, they sweat like crazy, of course, and the work they do is hard physical stuff."

"Yes," Lilly said.

"This is a simple set-up here," he said, "but we have everything essential that we need. It's been very well planned and organized. These guys sure know what they're doing. We can learn a lot from this."

Lilly nodded.

Several hours later, tired and hungry, Lilly made her way back to her tent for a rest before going for the evening meal in the community centre. As she walked, she found herself staggering a little from fatigue, yet her mind was churning, on high alert. She hoped that the tent would be empty as she felt the need to be alone, to think about the unexpected appearance of Rafe and to lie down and close her eyes.

Thankfully, the tent was empty, bathed in a soft green light from where the sunlight filtered through the canvas. Someone had set up a large electric fan to cool the interior, which would otherwise have been unbearably hot. As it was, she was sweating with the summer heat. The fan made a soothing, faint swishing noise.

The young corporal, Jessie Kemp, had left her camp

bed tidy, the blanket neatly folded, her rucksack underneath.

With her shoes off, Lilly lay on her camp bed, which was surprisingly comfortable, with her arm flung across her eyes to shut out the light. As much as she needed to sleep, she needed to sort out her emotions with regard to Rafe. It was very obvious that her feelings for him had not changed. In fact, they seemed to be taking on a new and more powerful dimension as the absence—and now the new setting— allowed her to see him in a new light. In this place she could see him as the multi-faceted, complex person that he was, as well as the skilled surgeon and compassionate doctor that she knew him to be. And he had kissed her.

Lilly stirred restlessly, moving her head from side to side, as though to shake off a bad dream. What were they going to do? A way forward seemed no easier than it had done months before. Perhaps if he had asked her to marry him because he wanted to and not out of obligation, things would have been different. She did not doubt for one moment that he had suggested marriage from a sense of duty.

"Lilly! Lilly!" A voice brought her back, sluggishly, into consciousness. "Wake up and get up."

"What?" she muttered.

"It's me—Ashley. It's time for supper. And there's to be an information session by one of firefighting guys to us greenhorns about fires."

"Oh, God," Lilly groaned, opening her eyes and then closing them again, flinging her arm across her eyes. "I'm tired."

"Sit up," Ashley said. "I've brought you a mug of tea, and we have a container of water here, plus a bowl and a bucket, so that we can wash our face and hands without having to go over to the mess all the time."

"Great," Lilly said, forcing herself to wake up, sit up and put her legs over the side of the camp bed and plant them firmly on the ground. "Things are catching up with me—the journey up here and everything. Thanks for the tea, Ashley. Just what I need."

"You're welcome. We have to get over to the mess in about fifteen minutes for supper. The talk is going to be delivered while we eat, to save time."

As she sipped her tea, Lilly noted the large clear plastic container of water nearby, which had a tap on it. There was a plastic bowl and a bucket for the waste water. "Is that water drinkable?" she asked.

"It is."

She noticed that Jessie had rigged up a small mirror on the tent wall near her camp bed, so she got up and stared into it, noting that her short, fine dark hair was standing up at all angles, that her face was flushed from sleep and the effects of the sun that day. Her large blue eyes had a haunted expression, with shadows under them, as they stared back at her sombrely from her heart-shaped face, which was devoid of any sort of artifice. Raking a hand through her hair, she tried to collect her thoughts.

While Lilly washed her face and hands from the plastic bowl full of cold water, Ashley chatted about what she had been doing. "What's the story between you and Dr Neilson, if you don't mind me asking?" she suddenly said. "Tell me to shut up if you want to."

"It's all right," Lilly said, drying herself on a towel that she had brought with her from Albertstown. "To put it in a nutshell for you, we worked together, then lived together. It would take too long to explain why we're no longer living together. Just one of those things. I'll tell you about that some other time."

The details of her personal life were not things that she wanted to divulge to someone she didn't know very well. Although she was coming to feel that Ashley was a friend, it was a little soon, and Rafe himself might not appreciate having his personal life aired to others. "He was the last person I expected to see here," she went on, "so it's all a bit strange."

"Mmm," Ashley said ruminatively. "It must be. He seems like a really nice guy."

"He is. There were some family problems. We…we needed a break from each other. I felt I wasn't sure of him…and to give him a chance to get away from me, if that was what he wanted." She struggled to explain, as much for herself as for Ashley.

Now that weeks had gone by, and confronted by the

unexpected presence of Rafe here, she found herself less sure of her motives and her reasoning at the time. All she had understood then had been that she had needed to be on her own for a while in order to think clearly.

"Oh. It sounds as though he wanted to get away from the city as well. It's really amazing that you should have fetched up in the same place," Ashley said.

"Yes."

"If I had a nice guy like that look at me the way he looks at you, I would grab him," Ashley said.

"He looks at me angrily," Lilly said, surprised.

"Yeah, but there's something else underneath," Ashley said. "Something worth having."

Flushing, Lilly hid her emotions by busily getting ready to leave the tent. "I know he used to care for me," she said quietly. "And I care for him. But I really don't know what he thinks about me now."

When they were both freshened up and cleaned up in a superficial way, they walked over to the community centre, which was now the mess, and lined up with others for a meal. Lilly looked around quickly for Rafe, not seeing him.

What she could not tell Ashley right now was that she had been pregnant, was still devastated about the loss of her child. Not even Rafe understood the full extent of that. At the time, as well as afterwards, she had wondered whether the shock and upset of having been accused of underhand tactics had brought about the chain of events and the sense of deep mourning and depression that had come over her. It would be a relief to unburden herself to someone as sensible and mature as Ashley—eventually.

''There's Rafe,'' Ashley said, as she and Lilly sat down with their plates full of food at one of several trestle tables. ''Shall I ask him to join us?''

Lilly shrugged, as though she didn't care, while Ashley went over to Rafe who was in the line for food.

''Hi,'' he said to her when they were all seated. His dark blond hair was wet. ''I've heard this talk before, but it bears repeating.''

''It's great for us to have you here, Dr Neilson,'' Ashley said, ''to pave the way for us, so to speak.''

Lilly said nothing, merely nodding, very conscious of his presence as she bent over her plate of food. He sat down next to Ashley, who began to converse with him chattily, as though she sensed Lilly's mood of confusion and was covering up for her.

As they ate, a very tired-looking, middle-aged fire-fighter stood up to address them.

''Listen up, you guys,'' the firefighter began, grinning at them in an attempt to lighten the mood. ''I won't keep you too long, as I know some of you are itching to get back to the smoke, while some others are dying to have a beer and a good sleep.'' There was a ripple of laughter at his words.

''This session is aimed at those who have never

been in the vicinity of a forest fire before, and essentially don't know much about them," he went on.

"That's me, for sure," Ashley muttered.

"This army camp," the man said, "is under the direction of Sergeant Major Gregson. I'm with the fire department myself, not with the army. We are all under the direction of the fire chief, who has the final word in the firefighting plan."

As Lilly listened and paused in eating her meal, she was very aware of Rafe sitting close to her, aware of a tension that seemed to emanate from him, which she interpreted as animosity towards her.

"High winds and lightning," the firefighter went on, "are the enemies of firefighters battling fires. There can be hundreds of lightning strikes in twenty-four hours. A shift in wind direction can blow a fire quickly towards built-up residential areas."

"You know all this already, do you?" Ashley whispered to Rafe.

He made a wry face. "My knowledge is rudimentary," he said.

Lilly looked away, trying to concentrate on the information, which was interesting and dramatic in its understatement.

As the audience listened, they were mainly silent, very aware of the fires that raged not too far away, conscious of the all-pervading scent of smoke and the need to be vigilant because the situation could change dramatically in a very short space of time. There was an air of unreality about it, yet at the same time it was so immediate that the feeling of hyper-awareness never left them.

Mentally, Lilly went over the emergency procedure for the umpteenth time, picturing herself running to the tent where the patients were, with the siren shrieking in the background, getting them onto the buses, helping others pack up the boxes of drugs and other essential supplies and equipment that could not be left behind. Other army personnel would take down the tents, load them into trucks. Then she would run to her own tent to get her bags...

Lilly found herself looking around for the exits from the large hall, the escape routes. Here at this temporary army base they were not safe, no one in the community was safe. Someone had to be constantly vigilant on their behalf so that they were not cut off from the airstrip and escape.

How strange it felt to be in actual physical danger. How would she behave, Lilly speculated soberly, when, or if, it came to the crunch? Between them and disaster, in the here and now, was a thin, dedicated line of brave and experienced firefighters and soldiers, men and women whose job it was to put their lives on the line to protect others.

"Listen up!" Rafe said. "As they say in the army. I can tell your mind's wandering."

When she cast him a sceptical glance, he added, "I know you pretty well."

Was he softening towards her, she wondered, or was that comment for Ashley's benefit?

"So you think," she whispered back huffily. The depression was on her again, like a cloud. She had wanted that child, had longed for it...

"A fire can burn underground, in tree roots," the firefighter went on.

How like human emotions that was, Lilly thought. The past that seemed dead was not really dead. It could be brought to smouldering life, given the right conditions.

"These are called 'smokers'," the man said. "The men have bags of water strapped to their backs, each with a hose, to help douse the smokers. The soldiers call these 'piss cans'."

There was general laughter, a momentary release of tension. Perhaps I ought to be taking notes, Lilly thought, then thought that, no, she didn't need to, because she would remember every word of this, maybe for the rest of her life.

"While we're using these piss cans, we pray for rain," the firefighter joked. "So if you meet a guy talking to himself, with one of those things strapped on his back, and a hose in his hand, that's what he's doing—praying."

There was laughter again, a lightening of mood.

The firefighter went on for half an hour, then fielded questions, while some of them went to the serving hatch for tea or coffee.

"World Aid is very sensible to send us to a place like this first," Lilly commented as she sipped tea. "This is our country. At least we have a good sense of the way things are done."

"Yeah," Ashley said. "Imagine being this scared in a remote, primitive place. Although this place is pretty remote, I guess."

"You may well find yourself this scared in a remote, primitive place," Rafe said dryly.

"I think I would be checking our escape routes constantly," Lilly said.

They took their seats again, while the firefighter positioned himself at the front again, clearing his throat in preparation for speech.

When the talk was over, Lilly felt somewhat dazed from the information she had absorbed.

When they were outside in the warm summer air, tinged as always with smoke, the army doctor who had worked with Ashley earlier came up to them. "Could you three guys do an evening shift up to, say, ten o'clock? I've got two airlifts to supervise. I want to go to the airstrip with them."

All three nodded. "Sure," Rafe said, speaking for all of them. The food they had just eaten had temporarily cancelled out their fatigue.

"Ms Soper, if you could go to tent two as before, and the other two of you to tent one, as before, that would be great," the doctor said. "You'll find an orderly in each one."

"Right," Lilly said. It was all deadly serious, yet seemingly casual at the same time. She found that she had the utmost confidence in those around her, which inspired her to do her very best in professional terms.

In their tent they found four patients on camp beds, under the care of the orderly, who quickly brought them up to date. Three of the patients were having intravenous fluids because of dehydration, one of whom was also on oxygen for smoke inhalation. The fourth patient had superficial burns, as well as being in need of fluid, so also had an IV running.

Lilly and Rafe changed quickly into clean scrubs and washed their hands very thoroughly.

"We need the vital signs done on all these guys," the orderly said to Lilly, "and the charts brought up to date. It would be great if you could do that. I want your opinion, Dr Neilson, on the burns case. He has asked not to be shipped out, but I think he ought to go if he needs skin grafts. He won't be able to go back to work fighting fires right now, that's for sure. These guys hate to give up. They know there often isn't any-one to take their place."

The orderly, John, drew them aside to express con-cern about the approaching fires.

"Judging by the stronger smell of smoke in the past little while, I think the fires are getting closer to us, so make sure you know the evacuation protocol. We may not get much warning. Three of these guys can get on the bus by themselves, but the guy with the burns should not be putting weight on his leg with the burn. We've got a couple of wheelchairs here.''

''We'll keep that in mind,'' Lilly said, with a thrill of fear, trying not to let it show on her face. ''I'll get on with the vitals, shall I?''

''Sure. Thanks. I sure appreciate having you guys here,'' John said. ''Just a few words of warning. In my experience, most things of an emergency nature in the field take longer to accomplish than you think they're going to, so have a good plan for what you personally have to do. At least one vital thing tends to go wrong…I think that's Sod's Law, eh?''

''Something like that,'' Rafe said, grinning. ''There's a law for just about every situation. If something can go wrong, it will.''

''Sure thing,'' John said. He was a plump young man, tall and big with it, with a deceptively boyish and easygoing demeanour. Lilly suspected that he would be wonderful in an emergency, steely and ultra-efficient, the type of guy who put his life on the line without thinking about it.

Both she and Rafe had read the emergency protocol several times.

Some of the fear she felt subsided as she went through the familiar routine of taking the patients' blood pressures, their pulse rates and temperatures and recording the results on their charts, while Rafe conferred with John regarding the burns.

Someone had brought food from the mess for the

men, and now a volunteer came to pick up the used trays and crockery. After she had taken the vitals and charted them, Lilly checked the intravenous lines and the bags of fluid, making sure the fluid was dripping at the designated rate. Two of the bags were almost empty, so she searched through a plastic box of IV bags to find the litre bags of saline for replacement.

It was almost midnight before Lilly was able to leave the treatment tent, to go out into the night, which was redolent with the products of combustion. It had been one of the most unusual days of her life, leaving her disorientated. Although very tired, she had the feeling that she would not be able to sleep well.

"I want to talk to you," Rafe said, close behind her. "Come to my tent. I happen to have a small tent to myself."

"Not one we have to crawl into, I hope," she said.

"No."

"What do you want to talk about? I'm awfully tired."

"So am I," he said curtly. "Since we are here in the same place, we may as well get a few things sorted out. There might not be other opportunities, if we get evacuated from here."

As they set out, the path illuminated by a flashlight that Rafe was holding, they saw a figure approaching though the gloom, and recognized Jessie Kemp.

"Hi, there!" Jessie said, stopping beside them on

the dirt path. "How's it going with you guys? I wanted to ask you earlier, but didn't get much of a chance. I've just had a bit of sleep, now I'm back on night duty, fire-watching. I have to say, it doesn't look too good for this community. If the wind veers around a bit more this way, we may have to get out."

"That bad?" Lilly asked, trying to sound casual.

"Yep. If I were you, I wouldn't undress. Keep your boots handy and have all your gear ready to go," Jessie said. "Have your water bottle full."

"Is it safe to go to sleep?" Lilly asked, wondering if Jessie would notice that her voice was high-pitched with fear. "Not that I feel as though I can sleep."

"Oh, I reckon it's OK to sleep. The siren will wake you up all right if we have to get out," Jessie said. "Well, have to go. You take care now. Watch out for each other, you two and your other buddy. That's the best way."

"Sure," Rafe said. "You take care, too, Jessie."

"Will do. 'Night."

"Come on." Rafe took Lilly's arm. "This way."

His tent was actually quite large, you could actually stand up in it. "How come you rate a tent like this?" Lilly said when they were inside it. "This is very civilized." She looked around to cover up her tension, at the neat camp bed with the pillow and blanket, his gear stacked in a corner, the water bag and bowl.

"I guess I don't fit neatly into a particular category,'' he said. ''I'm a doctor, but not with the army. They want to make me feel comfortable.''

All at once there was an electrifying tension between them as they stood looking at each other in the glow of the flashlight that he still held.

''I…'' Lilly looked around her wildly. ''Shall I put that light on?'' she asked, looking at a small battery lamp that was on an upturned box beside his camp bed.

''No,'' he said quickly, ''don't put it on. It will silhouette us against the canvas, visible from the outside.''

''Does it matter?'' she asked, her voice high with tension. It had been a mistake to come here with him.

He clicked off the flashlight, plunging them into complete darkness.

''Why did you do that?''

''Now we find ourselves together,'' he said, ''we may as well get a few things sorted out. For a start, why have you been avoiding me, not answering my phone calls, always being out, back in Toronto and then in Albertstown?''

''We agreed that we would not contact each other—''

''Correction,'' he said. ''You said that. I did not agree. You've treated me like some sort of pariah.''

''No…''

''Yes,'' he said harshly. ''I want to know what I've done to deserve that. Tomorrow I'm going to contact

World Aid and get you shifted out of here because, as I said, I don't think I can work with you.''

"Don't do that," she protested. ''The way things seem to be going, we'll both be out of here soon enough. Put the light on.''

"No," he said. ''And keep your voice down, otherwise we'll have an audience.''

"I…'' She blundered into him. ''Let me out of here.''

In a moment he was holding her against him tightly, his hands on her upper arms.

"Don't," she protested, fearing that if he kissed her she would not be able to leave him…and she didn't think she was ready for that, and neither was he. With the anger that she sensed in him, he would just be using her…

Lilly pushed him away. ''Why are you so angry with me?'' she asked brokenly. ''I'm the one who had the miscarriage.''

"But I am not responsible, I did not make it happen," he said. ''I have a sense that you blame me. Otherwise, why would you up and leave the way you did?''

"I came to the conclusion that I don't belong in your world," she said.

"Don't give me that," he said savagely. ''How can I trust you, or believe anything you've told me? I feel for you, I understand about the baby. But I didn't make it happen.''

At some point she would have to tell him about the visit from his step-family. Somehow the words stuck in her throat. It all went together with being taunted as being "trash" at school. If only she didn't care so much, if only she could brush it aside as it deserved to be. Perhaps at some time in her life, perhaps when she was middle-aged, it would cease to matter. She assumed that there was a time in your life when you just accepted yourself, liked yourself for who you were, didn't care much what other people thought of you.

The sound of trucks arriving at the camp diverted them, brought them back to a state of hyper-alertness, and they stood listening. Rafe switched on the flashlight and sat down on the bed, in expectation of being called. There was to be little or no sleep.

Before long, hurrying footsteps came along the gravel path to the flap of the tent.

"Dr Neilson?" a man's voice enquired.

"Yes?" Rafe called out.

"Sorry to call you, but we've got a new contingent of injured. Could you come?"

"Sure. I'll be there in less than three minutes."

"Thanks, Dr Neilson." The footsteps receded.

To Lilly, it felt even more as though they were in a war zone as she listened to the sound of trucks coming and going. Everything felt urgent, fraught with danger, overlaid as it was by the oppressive heat.

There seemed no way to predict what would happen next.

"Take my flashlight," he said, "to find your way to your tent."

"I've got one of my own, thanks," she said.

There was no doubt in her mind that tomorrow he would contact World Aid. She stood awkwardly, waiting for him to go first.

"I'll see you in the morning," he said, his voice more gentle than it had been earlier in the day, but still not quite right, she thought. After a hesitation, when she thought he was going to bend to kiss her, he touched her face briefly, then abruptly unzipped the tent flap and went out.

With his touch warm on her face, she let tears flow down her cheeks as she stood in the tent, comforted in a bitter-sweet way by the sense of his presence in the confined space, where his few belongings were scattered around. What was she to do? She still loved him, wanted to be with him. It was unlikely that he would ask her to live with him again. And she wasn't sure that the uncertainty of that was what she wanted. It seemed even more unlikely that he would ever ask her to marry him. Even if he were to do so, she did not know whether she would have the confidence to accept.

There was a wind in the trees just outside the tent, normally a soothing sound but the enemy of the firefighters; there were sounds from the comings and goings of the camp farther away.

When, a few minutes later, she let herself quietly into her own tent she found that Ashley was asleep, curled up on her camp bed, fully clothed except for her shoes. By the light of the flashlight Lilly went up to her camp bed, noticing as she did so that Jessie had folded up her own camp bed, had put her rucksack neatly beside it, together with the folded blanket.

The sight of that folded camp bed was somehow disturbing to Lilly, who suspected that Jessie had folded it up so that it would be easier for the men to cart away if they had time to dismantle the tent if a fire approached. Those tents were worth thousands of dollars and would not be left behind if there was any time to dismantle them.

Very quietly she had a quick wash and brushed her teeth, with the aid of the bowl and water bag. Then she packed up all her gear, putting her heatproof boots and the newly issued fireproof clothing on top of it, where she could put her hands on it quickly.

After easing off her shoes and socks from her aching feet, she lay down on the camp bed, her flashlight beside her right hand. Her mind was in a whirl, literally and emotionally. There were distant, muted sounds, men shouting, engines starting up, not loud enough to be disturbing. What was disturbing was an increasing sound of wind in trees, not far from the tent.

Shutting her eyes, she tried to relax. Must get some sleep…

Nonetheless, her mind was active. Perhaps here and now, in this place of danger, she would somehow find it easier to tell Rafe about recent happenings, as well as about her less than affluent childhood…if she got the chance. It was that very danger, she assumed, that concentrated the mind wonderfully. Perhaps he would understand that she had had a crisis of self-confidence, particularly after she had lost the baby, her one true link to him.

# CHAPTER FOUR

IT WASN'T difficult to get up when the first light of dawn penetrated the green canvas of the tent, when the camp bed began to feel less than comfortable. Lilly found herself wide awake.

She grabbed her toilet bag and towel and made her way over to the mess to have a shower before the general rush, leaving Ashley still asleep. A lot of people didn't appear to sleep around this place, so it was a privilege to lie down for more or less a whole night. The firefighting activity, the medical care and first aid, went on twenty-four hours a day.

It felt like a luxury to stand under a cool shower on the warm, humid morning, to rub shampoo into her hair, to wash out the sweat that had accumulated on her scalp. Already the facilities of a comfortable, civilized world could not be taken for granted in quite the same way. As she dried herself and put on clean clothes, she wondered whether Rafe would be up yet. The mess served food around the clock. No doubt they would be serving breakfast already, so she decided to go now, looking forward to a cup of coffee and some orange juice.

Dumping her toilet articles on a chair in the corner

of the big hall-cum-mess, she went up to the serving hatch where two firefighters, filthy in their soot-covered gear, were getting breakfast, huge plates of pancakes and hash browns, smothered with maple syrup.

"Hi," Lilly said to them shyly, rather self-consciously running a hand through her damp hair as she lined up for food. "How are things going on the other side of the lake? I'm one of the World Aid volunteers." When she had last enquired about the fire, she had been told that it was ferocious, but still mainly on the other side of the lake.

"Hi, how ya doing?" one of them said to her, while the other nodded a greeting. "It ain't too good, because it's on this side of the lake now. We're doing our best, but she's a bummer. The wind has not been in our favour, I can tell you. Stay close to camp, that's my best advice. We try to give you an hour's notice before you have to get out, but you never know the way things will go. It's just an educated guess."

Lilly helped herself to coffee, juice, cereal and fruit, declining the huge spread that the men were consuming. They needed it more than she did, with the vast amount of energy they were expending. Four kitchen staff cooked and doled out the food with cheerful expertise.

The coffee was some of the best she had ever tasted. Lilly planted her elbows on the Formica-topped table, closed her eyes and sipped from the mug, holding it in both hands. All was deceptively quiet and peaceful in these moments before proper dawn. At last she could gather her thoughts into some sort of coherent form, about World Aid and her future with the organization, about Rafe Neilson. It was good to be in the vast room with only two other people. She could at last hear herself think.

A few other people wandered into the mess hall, then Rafe came, as she had half hoped he would.

"Hi," he called, striding over to her as soon as he saw her, a slightly cynical smile on his face, or so it seemed to her. "How is the fair Lilly?" At least he was still speaking to her off duty. It wasn't in his nature to be boorish, what ever else he might be feeling where she was concerned right now. They had to work together, until he did his utmost to get her shifted out.

"So-so," she said, playing it cool. "This is great coffee."

In his fatigues he looked businesslike, and very, very attractive and fit, every inch a man, and she found her eyes going over him possessively, over his taut muscles, his lean, hard body. As though she had a right to him, she discovered.

Like her, he had obviously just had a shower, his hair wet, his face scrubbed clean. With all that, he looked haggard, as though he had not slept much.

While he was getting his food, she decided that she

would not say anything about his intention to call World Aid.

In moments he was back with a tray of food. After a mouthful of coffee, he looked at her, his eyes going over her face, as though he had not looked at her properly since she had arrived there. "We should take this opportunity to get a few things sorted out," he said. "There isn't much time. Apparently the fire is now well and truly on this side of the lake. If we get evacuated, I'd like to know where you are."

"Really?" she said. "I've been getting the impression that you couldn't wait to see me disappear over the horizon." It seemed, in this unlikely place, that she was getting glimmerings of her sense of humour back.

He chose to ignore that. "It will be crazy, getting our patients and ourselves out. For my peace of mind, I'd like to know that you're safely at the airstrip."

"And where will you be?" she asked. "I assume that you'll be safely at the airstrip too, so you'll see me there."

"I expect I will be," he said. "We should have a plan A, which will be to meet at the initial mustering point, outside this building. If, for whatever reason, we miss each other here, we'll go to plan B, which will be to see each other at the airstrip."

"And what if we don't see each other there?" she asked.

"I shall not get on a plane until I know where you are," he said.

"The same applies to me," Lilly said. "I don't think I would want to get out if I didn't know where you were."

"Curious, isn't it?" he said. "You wanted to get out of my life, but you wouldn't leave me here."

"Well, I...I don't hate you," she said, not looking at him. "Is there a plan C?"

"I haven't thought of one yet."

More people came into the vast room, including Ashley who came over to them. "Hey, you guys," she said. "What's this getting up before dawn bit?"

"Just raring to go." Lilly smiled, trying to keep a tremor out of her voice. "Get yourself some food and join us, Ashley."

"I've just been told that one of the firefighters is going to take us on a quick tour of the community before we have to start work," Ashley said excitedly, "so that we can be more orientated. He's going to take us as close to the fires as we can safely get, so that we can have a better idea of what we're up against. We have to muster in about fifteen minutes outside the mess."

"Good," Rafe said. "I want to see how far away the fires are from us."

"Same here, although maybe it's better if we don't know too much," Ashley said, with a rueful laugh. "The smell of smoke has sure got stronger, and the visibility right now is not as good as it was yesterday. I folded up our camp beds, Lilly, just in case, following the example of Jessie.''

Lilly nodded and stood up. ''I'd better take my stuff back to the tent. See you guys in fifteen minutes.''

There were eight of them at the mustering point, a good number to fit comfortably into the truck that was there to transport them. First they went to the community of Crater Lake, which was like a ghost town. The sun was rising, gaining warmth, to add to the heat already in the air. A haze hung over the main street of small buildings and the few shops that made up the commercial area. Small streets of unpretentious houses ran at right angles to it, away from the lake. Soot and bits of ash had coated everything. There were no people in sight.

''A burnt-out area can look like a war zone,'' the driver said. ''Thankfully, we haven't got to that point yet here. We hope to save the homes here and the other buildings. This place was evacuated some time ago.''

''What about the pets?'' Lilly asked.

''We got those out, too.''

The community bordered on the lake from which it got its name, a large body of water. In the early morning haze and smoke they could see far out onto the water, but not to the other side, which they knew had been devastated by fire. When the truck stopped, so that they could get a closer look at the lake, the silence was eerie. Not for the first time, the power of natural forces, fire this time, made its presence felt.

Tuning into their thoughts, the driver said, ''You have to respect fire, be prepared for it, as everything powerful in nature, otherwise it will get you. There were forest fires here long before man appeared on the scene. If you build a house in a forest, sooner or later you'll get burned out. It's a law of nature.''

Along the shore of the lake were several wooden jetties at intervals. There was a small marina, with a few motorboats and some wooden boats tied up there, left by their owners who were perhaps still in the area as volunteers. Some boats, they could see, had been taken out into the lake and anchored there.

''There are a few people who volunteered to stay here to keep a fire vigil,'' the driver said, ''around the clock. That's very stressful.''

The driver turned the vehicle around and they went back in the opposite direction, past the community centre and the camp, towards the fires. They drove along a road, an extension of the main street, which was paved for the first few hundred yards, then turned into a dirt road going off towards the forest.

Indeed, there was forest all the way round this community, pressing in on it, except where the lake came up to the main street, forming a barrier against fire. Yet the flames had come round the edge of the lake, had roared through the forest not far from the edge of the community. As Lilly looked around her curiously, she began to feel somewhat claustrophobic, seeing the tall trees, mostly conifers, very close to the road, separated from it by a ditch on either side.

As they rounded a shallow bend in the road the density of smoke was suddenly thicker and the smell of it penetrated the vehicle.

Before long they came to a metal barrier across the road and were flagged down by a soldier. ''Hi,'' he said, planting his elbows on the edge of the window that the driver had opened. ''Who might you be, sir?'' He carried a clipboard and had a pen stuck behind an ear.

''We're from the community centre mess and army base. Volunteers. This is an orientation trip, so that we can get some idea of what's going on. May we go through?''

''Not with the vehicle you can't,'' the soldier said, motioning them over to a grass verge, while he laconically took the pen from behind his ear. ''We have to keep this road clear as an escape route for the fire-fighting guys. Park over there and you can go in on foot. Only don't go more'n a couple o' hundred yards. Be back here in no more than fifteen minutes.''

''Right,'' the driver said. ''Thanks, bud. No sweat.''

As they all got out of the truck, the scent of the smoke was strong, while it seemed to press down on them like a cloud as they stood in the centre of the dirt road. Confetti-sized pieces of ash floated eerily around them. The soldier presented the clipboard to the driver.

"Print and sign your name there, sir," he said. "And write down all the other names, if you please, and state where you're from, all of you. We have to account for everyone here. We don't want missing persons."

"Right."

Lilly found that her heart was beating fast when the formalities were over and they were on the other side of the barrier. Her fatigues were sticking to her with sweat.

"There's a vantage point a little ways up," the soldier called to them, "round the next bend, a bit of a hill. You'll see about all you need to see from there."

"Thanks."

It was very quiet as the eight of them moved forward, their footfalls making no sound on the dry dirt. Only the slight rustle of their clothing disturbed the silence. They could see how dry everything had become in the drought, as their shoes disturbed dry soil and sent up small clouds of dust. Tall stalks of brown grass beside the road stood like dead sentinels.

"Makes you realize what those guys are up against, doesn't it?" Ashley said to Lilly and Rafe, as the three of them walked abreast. "Look at the density of those trees."

"Yes. I don't mind admitting I'm scared," Lilly said.

Before they had gone far, the silence was broken by the whop, whop, whop sound of helicopter rotors, coming nearer. Looking up, they saw the helicopter with a huge bucket slung underneath it, held by a long cable.

"They bring in water from the lake so that the guys fighting the fire on the front line can replenish their water supply," the driver of the van said. "And that plane's a water bomber just coming up over there." He pointed to an aircraft that had just come into view. "They get water from the lake too and drop it directly, just ahead of the fires if they can. It's a very dangerous job, because those flames shoot real high, and the planes have to fly low to be effective. Some planes drop fire-retardant chemicals as well."

When they rounded the bend from where the soldier had said there would be a vantage point, there were gasps and exclamations from the party.

Lilly put her hand involuntarily up to her mouth in the universal gesture of shock and surprise.

Ahead of them and to the right, where the lake came to an end, there was a raging inferno of fire, leaping high into the air, the flames looking like masses of waving arms. From where they stood they could hear it roaring and the air was decidedly hotter.

Above the flames was a dense pall of black smoke that had moved also down into a shallow valley to their right at the head of the lake, obscuring the view.

At the base of the fire, the orange-red glow was intense.

From where they stood, they could see a few tiny figures of firefighters in the distance. They saw vehicles, fire trucks, holding equipment and no doubt waiting to take the men out if they had to retreat from the danger zone.

"Those guys have to be careful they don't get ringed by fire," the driver said. "The whole scene can blow up in their faces. They can get a huge flash fire, where suddenly everything in an area is on fire, in spite of their efforts. You can imagine the heat…and it uses up all the oxygen right there. That's called a firestorm, and all the guys can do then is get out, if they can. Sometimes they have to get in their trucks and drive like hell through a wall of flame."

"Oh, God!" Ashley said. "I wonder how long this is going to take before it reaches the buildings."

"I think we've seen enough." Rafe voiced their thoughts, looking at his watch. "Our time's almost up, we'd better start back."

Sobered and frightened, and with many backward glances, they set off back the way they had come, until the bend in the road obscured the fire from them once again. Rafe, walking next to Lilly, brushed his arm against hers. "Remember plan B," he said very quietly, so that only she could hear. "I'll want to know where you are."

Squinting up at him in the harsh summer light, Lilly

nodded. "I'll want to know where you are as well," she said.

Two more helicopters moved towards the fire, while one moved back out, filling the sky with the sound of their rotors.

It was a relief to get back into the truck, which seemed like a sanctuary, a link between the unbridled power of nature and the civilized world that they were used to. Lilly had a few seconds of panic when she imagined what would happen if the engine would not start, if they had to walk back, if they were overtaken by the fire, suffocated by smoke.

The soldier at the barrier had a motorbike with him, as well some sophisticated radio and satellite telephone equipment.

"I'll drop you back at the camp," the driver said as they started up. "You can ask me any questions on the way."

"Thank you for taking us," Lilly said. "We have a much better idea of what we're up against now."

Back at the camp they went to their respective areas of work. It was still early.

Between the medic tents, Rafe pulled Lilly to one side. "Listen," he said urgently, "keep me informed of everything you're doing. I want to know where you are at all times."

"Why?"

"Because I do."

"Are you still planning to phone World Aid?" she asked, still not clear on that.

"As you said last night, we'll be out of here soon enough, by the look of that fire," he said. "If we're not out soon, I will call them."

"The army has a plan to get us out," she said. Now she had some intimation of what it would feel like to be separated from a "significant other", or a friend, in a crisis situation. Not knowing where they were would make you frantic with anxiety. Already, a slight sense of something like panic was feeling its way into her consciousness as Rafe voiced his concern. Having seen the fire close up, they knew where they stood. It seemed like a voracious beast, eating its way through the forest.

"Yeah, but it's easy to lose track of people in an emergency situation. Remember that we all have to sign out. Which reminds me, we had better sign back in again right now."

"Yes." They hurried back towards the mess. "We're not in control of the situation, Rafe," she reminded him. "We have to remember that in making any plans. We have to do what the fire chief dictates, go when and where he says."

"All the same, I want our own plan in addition to that."

There was a large sign-in, sign-out book on a table in the wide entrance passage of the community centre.

"You know, this all has an air of unreality," Lilly

said, as they signed their names, with the date and time, also stating where in the camp they would be. "Being here, finding you here…"

"It always does, in these sorts of situations," he agreed, "because you don't have time to get your head around what's happening. I guess you adapt with experience, learn to roll with the punches."

"There's also a feeling of dissonance…as though we ought to be somewhere else," she said.

"I know," he said. "We're used to emergency situations. There's no reason to think that we wouldn't or couldn't rise to the occasion. After all, a lot of the time we'll be doing what we normally do, more or less. We'll just be doing it under more difficult circumstances."

"Mmm." she said. "Our lives are not usually threatened."

There was a tension between them, of things left unsaid, of not knowing what to say, of the intense attraction that they had for each other. It wasn't an unpleasant tension, she considered. A quirk of fate, almost unbelievable, had brought them together in this remote place. They were two city-dwellers, facing raw nature, for which they were ill prepared.

"Lilly, I will not get on an aircraft without you," Rafe said. "Or without knowing where Ashley is. I'm in charge up here for World Aid."

Was he just stating his duty, she wondered, or could that mean that he still loved her? In this situation, it

# Play The *Lucky Hearts* Game

## and get...
# FREE BOOKS & a FREE GIFT...
# YOURS to KEEP!

*Yes!* I have scratched off the silver card. Please send me my **FREE BOOKS** and **FREE MYSTERY GIFT**. I understand that I am under no obligation to purchase any books as explained on the back of this card. I am over 18 years of age.

*Scratch Here!*
then look below to see
what you can claim...

M5EI

| Mrs/Miss/Ms/Mr | Initials |
| --- | --- |

BLOCK CAPITALS PLEASE

Surname

Address

Postcode

Twenty-one gets you
**4 FREE BOOKS** and a
**MYSTERY GIFT!**

Twenty gets you
**1 FREE BOOK** and a
**MYSTERY GIFT!**

Nineteen gets you
**1 FREE BOOK!**

**TRY AGAIN!**

## The Reader Service™ — Here's how it works:

NO STAMP NEEDED!

THE READER SERVICE™
FREE BOOK OFFER
FREEPOST CN81
CROYDON
CR9 3WZ

NO STAMP
NECESSARY
IF POSTED IN
THE U.K. OR N.I.

seemed almost too self-centred to be asking that question.

"That might be difficult in an emergency situation, when we have to do what we're told," she commented anxiously.

"Mmm," he said. "This situation is precisely why World Aid doesn't want people with emotional ties to work together. Already we're planning to step outside the framework they have set up."

"Do we have emotional ties still, Rafe?" she asked quietly.

"You answer that," he said brusquely.

As they were talking, it suddenly struck Lilly as odd that they should be planning not to be separated, when over the last few weeks she had wanted to be away from him.

"Can I get you guys a cup of coffee?" a voice enquired. One of the cooks had come out to the hall. "I've got a fresh brew on."

Lilly looked at her watch. "That would be great," she said. "It will have to be a quick one. Thanks a lot."

They stood by the serving hatch, drinking it, noting that the cook had a lot of his equipment and food packed up in large plastic boxes.

"We may not be here much longer," the cook said, seeing them eyeing the boxes, his manner matter-of-fact. "I get the very strong impression that things have deteriorated in the night. I also get very frequent news bulletins from up the front line.'' He gave a dry laugh.

"We got that impression, too," Rafe said, "although we know next to nothing about forest fires."

"There was a fair amount of wind up there in the night," the cook said. "Not good news."

"Thanks for the coffee," Lilly said as they departed.

"You're very welcome."

"We're cogs in the machine, Rafe," Lilly commented as they walked. "The protocol has been set out for our safety. It's going to be difficult to come up with our own plans."

"We are cogs that have to become machines in our own right if the machine breaks down," he said. "It's just so that I know where you are…and vice versa. Assuming that you want to know, that is?" There was an enquiring note with a touch of bitterness in his tone that stopped Lilly dead in her tracks.

"I do want to know—of course I do," she said.

"There's no 'of course' about it," he said. "One thing we have to keep in mind is that people…including ourselves…can behave in odd and unpredictable ways during extreme stress. And we often don't know how it's going to take us. That's why I want some of our own plans."

Without waiting for her to reply, he strode away from her so that she had to run to catch up. No doubt, he was partially referring to their present situation.

Without the previous personal stress in their lives, they would not be here, working in this remote place. The trick was to know yourself. Often it was only through difficulties and crises that you made leaps and bounds in knowing yourself. Then there was the task of knowing others…particularly that "significant other".

In the treatment tent they were met by John, who looked as though he had not slept for a long time. "Am I glad to see you guys!" he said effusively, surveying them with bloodshot eyes that had bags under them. "Would you take over while I get some coffee and do something about this beard?" He grinned tiredly, rasping a hand over a dense blond stubble on his lower face.

"Glad to," Rafe said.

"We've got a full house right now, mostly guys suffering from the heat. They came in during the night, so I couldn't get any shut-eye," John said. "There's an orderly here, name of Terry, who'll tell you what's what. We need some IVs put up and others changed. That's the top priority. Then there's a few superficial burns and some minor injuries to deal with. I won't be gone long. Sleep's a luxury right now."

When Rafe moved away to prepare for work, John took Lilly's arm to retain her. "What's with you two, if you don't mind my question?" he asked. "I sense pretty powerful vibes."

"We did know each other," she said. "It finished before we came and I had no idea he would be here."

"You'll get yourself sorted out here all right," John said, with a mirthless chuckle. "Being in a fire zone cuts through the crap."

"I'm beginning to see that," she said. "It's great working with you, John."

"Likewise. If you see Jessie, could you tell her I'll be over in the mess?"

"Sure."

"From what I've seen of him…" he jerked his head in the direction that Rafe had taken "…he's a great guy. My advice to you is loosen up," he added, grinning, departing before she could give any sort of come-back.

So much for thinking that your emotions were invisible to others, she thought ruefully as she prepared to start work.

In moments she had washed her hands, put on rubber gloves and joined Rafe in inserting intravenous lines in men who were lying on camp beds. The ability to tune out everything but the job in hand was a useful one, she thought as she attempted to clear her mind of everything else. It was not possible to erase the ever-present fear of the raging fires close by, the fear of hearing the siren.

At the head of each camp bed a clipboard hung from a hook stuck to the tent canvas, bearing notes about the occupant of the bed. This had to be taken down and the notes read quickly before any treatment could be undertaken. Most of the patients had a diagnosis of heat exhaustion and dehydration, a few had elevated temperatures—pyrexia of unknown origin—thrown in.

"What's it like up at the fire zone?" Lilly said, feeling somewhat fatuous as she asked the question of her first patient, Alec Ingram. "A few of us went up this morning to have a look from a distance."

"It's indescribable," he said, his eyes on the hand that she was cleaning with a soap solution prior to inserting an intravenous cannula. "To say that it's hell is an understatement. The heat and noise…the roaring of the flames, it's like a whole army of tanks coming at you. Sometimes you just want to run away, but you have to stick it out. It's your job."

"Yes," Lilly said. "I know the feeling."

To her, Alec Ingram was like a soldier who had just come off a battlefield, somewhat shell-shocked, a bit disorientated, very relieved to be out of the front line, like cases she had read about but never seen. Underneath the outward calm that he was struggling to maintain he was, she sensed, close to breaking point. On his face and neck were minor burns.

"You must be very hungry," she said, as she deftly inserted a fine intravenous "butterfly" cannula into a vein in the back of his hand. "This will take care of your fluid requirements and make you feel a lot better pretty quickly."

"I sure hope so," he said. "I've got the grandaddy of a headache. Someone told us that food's on the way. I'm starving."

"Good," Lilly said, adjusting the flow of the saline, having connected the intravenous tubing from the bag of fluid to the cannula. "I'll check up on that right now. You must be a volunteer firefighter."

"Yeah." He grinned wearily as he subsided back on his pillow. "I'm what you call a weekend firefighter. And I did volunteer. No one pushed me into it. This sure is a baptism by fire, in every sense."

Lilly bent down and squeezed his shoulder. "You just try to relax now," she said gently. "I'm going to chase up that food, then I'll be back in a while to take your blood pressure, pulse rate and temperature. I'll attend to those burns as well. Are you passing urine?"

"Yeah...I think so."

Lilly recorded the procedure on the clipboard chart, also making a mental note to bring him a urine bottle. Severe dehydration could damage the kidneys.

There was not much privacy in the tent. The men did not seem to mind that, they were so flat out with exhaustion that they had little energy to note what was going on around them. Each man seemed withdrawn into himself, no doubt extremely anxious about the safety of friends and colleagues that he had left behind at the front line of the fire.

"Terry, is food on the way for the men?" Lilly asked the orderly, having hurried to find him in the clean prep area.

"It'll be here any minute," Terry said, busy with

setting up more intravenous giving sets, connecting them to plastic bags of saline.

Lilly went back to tell Alec, then she planned her next move. The first priority was to get the intravenous saline running on all those patients who were suffering from heat exhaustion that John and Terry had not had time to get around to yet.

As she grabbed two more bags that Terry had prepared, she heard Rafe talking to a patient behind some makeshift screens. From what she could hear, the man had a fractured arm and some burns to face and neck. No doubt he would be flown out quickly, as he needed an orthopaedic surgeon.

Methodically she went around from patient to patient, putting in IV lines. Some of the men just lay there with their eyes closed, just acknowledging her presence with a mumble, signifying their exhaustion. A smell of fire clung to them, their hands were black with soot and dirt, the fingernails black.

Apart from cleaning a hand in preparation for the IV line and treating any abrasions or burns, it was pointless to attempt any clean-up. That would be done later when they had recovered, when they could have a shower, or it would be done at an outside hospital. The dirty state of the men made the place seem more than ever like a battle zone.

Back in the clean prep area to get some supplies for dressings and more bags, Lilly literally bumped into Rafe. ''How you doing?'' he said. At least he sounded neutral, instead of bitter, angry, or sarcastic—that was something. Although not clear on what she wanted from him, only knowing that she loved him, she found herself hoping that he would pursue her, as he had done at the hospital where they had met. It had been a wonderful, heady experience. Maybe it was not something that would happen twice.

"All right," she said. "I'm getting almost to like this frontier, battle-zone feeling, whatever you want to call it. It could be addictive once you get over the fear and strangeness of it."

"You're right," he said, standing close. "That's why we're with World Aid, presumably."

"Presumably," she said, just as Terry returned to the area. The young orderly was short and stocky, dressed in a green scrub suit that was now liberally darkened by patches of sweat.

"How you guys doing?" he said. "I sure appreciate having you here."

"We're just getting into the swing of it," Lilly said smiling at him. "I think." As she hurried away, the insight came to her again that the flurry of work, being able to feel really useful, had lifted her mood to the point where she felt closer to normal than she had felt for a long time. Being with Rafe again was part of it, she could see that now. Perhaps, more importantly, seeing this deserted community that was in very real danger of being consumed by fire forced her to put her own problems into a different perspective.

The people of Crater Lake had had to flee their homes with a few clothes, personal papers, some family photographs and other mementos. What would she take, she wondered, if she had been told that she must vacate her home in an hour's time, that what she left behind would probably be consumed by fire?

As she left the prep area she almost bumped into John, back from his ablutions, who voiced her thoughts. "I feel almost human again," he said, grinning at her, clutching a giant mug of coffee. "Maybe a week of sleep would complete the feeling."

"You look great." Lilly laughed, surveying his shaven face. Even though his eyes were still bloodshot, he looked refreshed. "And you smell absolutely delicious. Hope you don't attract too many mosquitoes."

"Naw," he said, smiling. "This stuff is guaranteed to draw the women and keep the bugs off. It's my cologne, called Summer Cool. You should try a bit of that, Dr Neilson," he added cheekily as Rafe stood by listening.

"It would take more than cologne to work for me," Rafe said, smiling.

"It's a start." John said. "Great things come from humble beginnings."

"Let's hope it works for you, then, John," Lilly said hastily, her cheeks pink. She liked the big, chubby, laconic trooper. "Shall I show you what I've done so far."

"Sure," he said.

Later, she went back to Alec Ingram, who had just finished eating from a small tray that he had perched on the side of his camp bed, while he lay sideways.

"I never knew orange juice and coffee could taste so good," he said.

"How's your headache now?" Lilly asked.

"A lot better," he said. "Not gone, though."

"I've brought you a urine bottle," she said. "I want to know if you can pass urine, that your kidneys are OK, for the record."

"OK," he agreed, watching Lilly as she dragged a makeshift privacy screen—fabric over a segmented metal frame on wheels—around his bed.

"Then I'll be back to look at those burns."

While she waited, she began her rounds again of the other men, checking the flow rates of the intravenous fluids, taking pulse rates, temperatures and blood pressures, writing her findings down on the charts.

John was doing the same thing, the fragrant scent of his cologne vying with the pervading smell of smoke and sweat that emanated from their patients' clothing. It was ironic, Lilly thought, smiling, that all his patients were men.

Alec managed to pass just enough urine to indicate that his kidneys were functioning, so she measured it and wrote the amount down on his chart, where she would also record the amount of fluid that he drank, as well as the amount of intravenous fluid going into him. Then she dressed his minor burns, recorded his vital signs and carried her used dressing tray out to the dirty prep area to clean it up.

As she, Rafe and John were standing near the entrance of the tent, a short, slight figure of a woman in uniform entered through the flaps, and Lilly recognized Jessie.

This time, more hair had escaped from her ponytail and was hanging down on either side of her elfin face. The face itself was dirty with soot, so that her blue eyes stood out startlingly like a summer sky. Her fatigues were somewhat the worse for wear, and she carried her firefighting clothes draped over one arm.

John was galvanized into added alertness at the sight of her. "Well, well, if it ain't Jessie," he said, going forward eagerly.

"What you on about?" she said stonily.

Rafe looked at Lilly, his lips twitching with suppressed laughter. Thank God we can still find something amusing, Lilly thought. Tentatively, she smiled back.

"What can I do for you, little darling?" John said, unperturbed.

"I'll tell you when I get my breath. How you doing, you big klutz?" she said, dropping her gear on the ground, breathing deeply.

"Better for seeing you," he said. "I manage."

Rafe came to stand close to Lilly. "Watch this

exchange,'' he suggested quietly, smiling. "You might learn something."

"Oh?" She raised her eyebrows. "And what about you? I'm not the only one who needs to learn something."

"You ought to be all right," Jessie said sourly to John, "safely here behind the lines, next to the food and medical supplies and all."

"I'm missing you," he said. "Don't you believe it's safe. Nowhere's safe in this place."

"Phoo-ee," Jessie said, coming closer. "What you got on you? Did you break a bottle of scent over yourself?"

"Just for you, babe," he said. "That's my cologne. Just to signify I'm clean."

Rafe looked at Lilly, raising his eyebrows and grinning.

"Oh, yeah?" she said. "That don't signify you're clean. More'n likely it's to cover up that you're not clean."

"I just had a shower. Cross my heart and hope to die if I ever tell a lie," he said.

Jessie giggled, brushing hair away from her grubby face with an equally grubby hand. Lilly busied herself in the nearby clean prep area, getting some dressings together. When Rafe came to stand beside her, it was all she could do not to reach out for him.

"We cracked up at the first hint of trouble, you and

I," he commented, causing her to look up at him sharply.

"I don't think you can put losing a baby in that category," she said.

"There are worse things, Lilly," he said soberly, the force of his stare making her sustain eye contact. "Like losing a child once it's born. It's time we came to terms with that."

"It's not that simple," she said bitterly.

"Of course it's not simple," he said. "It's a matter of degree."

"What gives, then, doll?" they heard John say. "Here I am, panting to help you."

Lilly swallowed to dispel the tight feeling of emotion in her throat. John had told her to loosen up. I'm trying, she thought, I'm trying. It wasn't helped by the underlying bitterness and something like anger that she sensed in Rafe, which was a barrier between them.

"First off," Jessie said, sniffing, "I got something heavy dropped on my foot. If I hadn't been wearing these boots, it would have broken every bone in my foot. Feels like it has, anyways. I want to get a bit of shut-eye, but the pain is killing me. Plus, I've a few minor burns here and there."

"What?" John said, in mock surprise. "With all that protective clothing you wear, on duty and off?"

"Shut up!"

"Disrobe behind them screens there, and I'll take a look," he said.

"I might just ask for a doctor," she said haughtily, "instead of a mere paramedic. You're free, aren't you, Dr Neilson?"

"I can be, Jessie," Rafe said carefully, "but I'm sure that in this situation John is much more of an expert."

The spell of bitterness was momentarily broken, and they all laughed.

"Dr Neilson's concerning himself with the dead and dying, not the walking wounded," John said glibly. "I can always get a consult, if you're adamant."

"What dead and dying? You'll be joining them if you put a foot wrong," she said. "Not to mention a hand."

"Wouldn't think of it," he said, putting an arm around her shoulders. "I'll give you something good to take the pain away so you can sleep."

"You'd better, otherwise I'm going to go absolutely nuts. You watch yourself, now," she said.

As he pushed through some privacy screens behind Jessie, John looked back at Lilly and winked. "See what I mean about the cologne?" he said. "Remember that—Summer Cool. Works every time."

"Come and do rounds with me, Lilly," Rafe said. "I want to make sure we haven't overlooked anything, and two heads are better than one in this situation."

"All right," she agreed. They began rounds, going to each man to assess his progress. Now she knew each man's case history and could relate it to Rafe without recourse to the chart, although she took down each chart to look at the input-output record and the other records of the vital signs. "There are a few fevers, some that can be accounted for, one or two that cannot."

They spoke and moved very quietly; if a man was sleeping, or just lying with his eyes closed, they did not disturb him. More than anything, these men needed to sleep. It was a very satisfying feeling, Lilly conceded, to look down the rows of camp beds in the shaded interior of the huge tent and see the fluid in the intravenous lines running as it should, the oxygen being administered to those who needed it—those who had suffered from smoke inhalation—and the clean dressings over wounds. All was in order, all was going well.

Yet it was an oasis in a desert. Not far away, the harsher reality prevailed. Before too long they might all be putting the disaster plans into action, saving their own lives and the lives of others. Even while they rested, there was a sense of alertness only slightly in abeyance, like that of a slumbering watchdog.

At Alec's bed, Lilly showed Rafe the intake and output chart. "He's passing urine, but maybe not enough," she said.

"Get him to void every half-hour," Rafe said. "If there's a significant discrepancy between his input and output, we may have to try him on an IV osmotic diuretic to get his kidneys up to par. We should keep a couple of bags hanging on the pole here, so that if we have to evacuate in a hurry we at least have the stuff available for him. The same applies to the saline and the dextrose.''

''Yes, I was thinking that,'' she said soberly. There was a superstitious feeling that by voicing such fears you made them happen. That was nonsense, of course, she thought with an odd shiver of apprehension. She reckoned that they had about an eighty per cent chance, at least, of having to evacuate.

At four in the afternoon, Ashley came into Lilly's work place. ''Hey,'' she said to Lilly, who was clearing up used dressing trays in the dirty prep area. ''Can you and Rafe come over to the mess for a cup of tea and a bun? Someone's going to be there soon, sorting out volunteers to be on fire vigil for the camp throughout the night. Yet another guy with a clipboard. It will be for two-hour stints throughout the night. I reckon we'll each have to do a shift, because there aren't enough people. Sleep's become a luxury.''

''Tea sounds great,'' Rafe said. ''We're about to get relieved by the incoming shift in this tent, so we'll be over there very soon.'' He put a hand on Ashley's shoulder. ''How are you, Ashley?''

''Running on adrenaline, like everybody else,'' she said ruefully. Her fair skin was paler than ever, her eyes shadowed. ''All I can say is that it's great experience. And that's what we came for, isn't it?''

"It is," he agreed. "See you over in the mess."

Seeing Rafe's hand on Ashley's shoulder gave Lilly a twinge of jealousy and a sense of possessiveness where he was concerned, and she turned away quickly lest it showed on her face. That emotion was a revelation to her, in more ways than one. By leaving him, she had forfeited the right of possession. His touch had been a friendly gesture, she sensed that, and she felt ashamed of her feeling, at the same time that she felt buoyed up by it. A deadness in her was shifting, gradually, towards a renewed life.

"See you, Ash," she said. "I feel as though we've been here two weeks instead of two days."

As soon as they were relieved, they left to go over to the mess. What a pleasure it was to sit down, to rest, feigning nonchalance, to cradle a large mug of tea in her hand, to sit opposite familiar faces.

John and Rafe sat opposite her and Ashley. On the table in front of them was a mound of sandwiches on a plate.

"This is sheer heaven," Lilly said, taking a mouthful of sweet tea. Quite a lot of people were milling about, getting food, taking a break.

"Help yourself to sandwiches," John said, pushing the plate around, "before I get my hands on them. I've been known to polish off this amount in one sitting."

"Listen up!" a voice said. It belonged to a sergeant who had come quietly into the mess. There was instantly a respectful silence. "This camp is now under a twenty-four-hour fire vigil, starting this evening. I need personnel who actually sleep in the camp to sign up now for two-hour stints throughout the night, starting at twenty-two hundred hours.''

Ashley and Lilly looked at each other. Silently they acknowledged that perhaps they were going to get at least part of what they had bargained for in terms of experience and excitement.

''There will be set beats that you will have to walk,'' the sergeant continued. ''You will have to keep a record and sign over to the incoming fire-watcher at the end of your shift. You will be given a pair of binoculars to help you spot fires, although for the most part you can see them when they're moving fast.''

No one else spoke. They all kept their eyes on the sergeant, each individual acutely aware of an increased tension in the room.

''You will have a flashlight and a portable phone, with a number to call to alert the fire marshal in town,'' he continued. ''There are fire-watchers all around the community. It will be your task to keep an eye on this camp. If the wind is blowing towards us, burning debris can blow for two kilometres or more, starting new fires where it comes down. You will watch for that debris and for new fires within your immediate vicinity. There will be a volunteer firefighting crew sleeping in this mess from now on, specifically for this camp. You, the fire-watchers, will inform them.''

He paused. The silence in the room was total. ''Raise your hands, please, all those who sleep here. OK. I want one person to take the twenty-two hundred to midnight shift.''

''I'll do it!'' Lilly called, waving her hand. Speaking broke the tension. If something was going to happen, bring it on. Waiting, trying to sleep, would perhaps be more stressful than fire-watching.

''Good.'' The sergeant strode over to her and looked at her and at her ID badge, with photograph, that she had pinned to a breast pocket. ''And your name, ma'am?''

''Lilly Page. I'm one of the nurses with World Aid.''

''Thank you, ma'am.'' He wrote her name down on a list. ''Stay here, have your tea. When I have the group together, in about fifteen minutes, we'll go outside for an orientation of the beat for the camp.''

Lilly nodded. ''Yes, sir,'' she said, not sure how to address him, feeling that he deserved a show of respect.

''I'd like to do the next shift, if I may,'' Rafe spoke up while the sergeant was still at their table. ''I'm Rafe Neilson, a doctor with World Aid.''

The sergeant looked at him astutely, eyeing his ID badge. ''Right. Thank you, sir,'' he said. ''Now, who will take the graveyard shift? No one likes that one because we're all dead beat by then. Any takers? Or do I have to say 'you, you, and you'? You can do the shifts in pairs if you want to, it's up to you. I don't want to run out of personnel, that's all. And, of course, I do want you to get some sleep.''

''Good for you,'' Rafe whispered to Lilly, his head close to hers, his words giving her a rush of pleasure. Already this place, this situation, was having a positive affect on her—it was forcing her to look outwards, as well as reassess her personal situation. She was scared, there was no doubt about that. Also, she knew now that she was very, very glad that Rafe was here with her. If he had been far away, she knew she would be contemplating maybe never seeing him again. There was little time now to analyse her feelings.

''I'll do that one,'' Ashley said, volunteering for the 2 a.m. shift, waving a hand. At the same time one of the army doctors also volunteered, one who had been working with Ashley.

''We'll do it together,'' he said, smiling at Ashley, who blushed, and there was general laughter and mild cheering.

''Thank you,'' said the sergeant.

# CHAPTER FIVE

THE night was hot and humid, made more oppressive by the even stronger scent of smoke that hung over the camp.

Having put on a T-shirt with her pants and some comfortable sneakers, Lilly emerged from the relative cool of the tent and felt a little as though she were entering a steam bath. On all exposed areas of her skin she had smeared insect repellent, as the night was replete with mosquitoes and other biting insects.

She had a bag slung from one shoulder across her chest, which contained the binoculars and cellphone. The large flashlight she held in her hand.

It was darkish and relatively quiet in the area of the tents where the personnel slept. Across the vast parking lot, up near the main road, she could see lights from vehicles and hear the sound of their engines. They would be firefighting and utility vehicles, going back and forth from the town and the camp to the fire zone.

Her beat would take her in a wide circle, around the backs of the billet tents, which were on the wide grass verge near the trees, up to the main road, then back behind the first-aid and medic tents. Beyond the main road, which went to the town on the right then up to the fire zone to the left, where they had been that morning, there was a sharp incline which provided a lookout to the fire zone. From there she would be able to see the glow in the sky. With the binoculars she could search out small new fires closer to the camp. Although those new fires might already have been spotted by other fire-watchers, she would get an idea of how close to the camp the real danger lay.

The first thing she had to do was rendezvous with Rafe at his tent, which they had agreed on earlier. She crossed the vast parking lot of the community centre, towards the tent where Rafe slept.

"Hey!" Rafe detached himself from the half-darkness as she approached. "Right on time."

"Of course," she said. "I hope you've smothered yourself with insect stuff, because this place is buzzing." Amazingly, they were talking to each other as though they didn't have any issues to resolve.

"I have," he said quietly. "I'm glad you're here. This feels like such an unreal situation. I keep asking myself if I'm mad, or what."

"Both, I expect," she said. "There's nothing like fear for your physical safety to make everything else more or less irrelevant, so I'm finding. It's funny, but somehow it feels right to be here...for me, anyway. Come on." The depressed, somewhat bitter person she had been a few days ago was, it seemed, being taken over again by her more normal self. There was no time to think too much about it. Besides, you could some-times think too much, not do enough.

Side by side, they began the beat, onto the grass verge, walking silently in their sneakers, starting on the wide circle that would take then round the camp, looking around them as they went. Lilly was very con-scious of Rafe next to her, of his large, masculine pres-ence, his familiarity, that she loved so much. When his arm inadvertently brushed against hers, she held her breath, expecting that he would take her into his arms…wanting him to. Instead, he kept walking, keep-ing up a steady pace.

"This place sure gives you a sense of urgency," he said.

"Yes," she agreed, careful to keep her voice down so that people inside the tents would not be disturbed. "It helps us to get our priorities sorted out."

They approached the main road, crossed it and walked up the long grassy incline opposite. Lilly could feel sweat trickling down her back, between her shoul-der blades, down from her armpits and on her face. At the highest vantage point they stopped and turned.

"Hell!" Rafe said. "It's closer. Look at that! My God!"

Struck dumb by the sight before them, over to their right now as they were turned facing the camp, Lilly felt her heart leap with that sickening sense of fear that one had when facing danger. It was not often in safe, civilized city life that you experienced actual physical danger, she realized. Most of that came from other human beings or from vehicles when crossing a street or driving, and that was tempered by the natural optimism that if you took basic, sensible precautions, the bad things would not happen to you. Here was the power of nature, fighting back against the puny efforts of man to tame it.

"I can hardly believe it." Awed by the sight before them, although safely in the distance at the moment, she knew it was probably only a matter of time before it reached them. "Oh, Rafe, I'm frightened." Lilly gripped his arm. "It's the impersonal nature of it that's so frightening."

Rafe turned to her and put his arms round her, as any decent human being might have done for another, and she put her head against his chest, her arms around his waist, allowing herself the comfort of his physical strength. "The sheer power of it," she said. "It's out of control, unless we get rain or the wind shifts."

"Yes." Then he bent his head and kissed her, as though it was the most natural thing in the world, because what they were facing was so far out of their control that all they could do was give each other that physical comfort. And she responded to him, closing her eyes, trying to blot everything else out of her consciousness for those few precious moments. It didn't matter whether it meant anything more than giving comfort. It didn't matter that he was bitter, that she was depressed. As they clung together, all she wanted was that precious confirmation that he felt as she did, understood and responded to her fear.

When they pulled apart they looked again at the glow in the sky above the fire. From where they stood they could see the flames shooting up, like tongues lapping at the night sky or many arms writhing in a macabre dance over a very wide area.

''It's definitely closer than it was this morning,'' she said, her voice high-pitched with nervousness. What she didn't want to voice was that it was a lot closer.

''I think we'll be evacuating pretty soon,'' Rafe said.

Clumsily, she pulled the binoculars from her bag and adjusted them as she looked through them so that she could sweep her vision over the areas between the fire and the camp. Small fires that had been started from smouldering debris might not be visible to them with the naked eye from this vantage point.

It took some time, and Rafe stood at her side in silence. They were both awed, reduced to their puny place in the grand scheme of things.

''I can't see any closer fires,'' she said when she had finished, lifting the strap of the binoculars from her body to hand them to Rafe. ''You should take a look. Maybe you can see something that I can't.''

Silently he took them.

''I felt dwarfed like this once before, by the power of nature or what ever you want to call it,'' she said, ''when my grandparents took me to the Rocky

Mountains when I was about eight years old. We went on some mountain trails by horseback. I felt so tiny and insignificant.''

''That pretty well sums us up when we're facing nature,'' Rafe said, making a slow sweep of the fire scene. ''Usually we're too arrogant to realize it.''

They stood side by side in silence while Rafe completed his scan.

''Even if it rains,'' she said, when he had finished, ''the man said it takes five days of rain to put out fires like this.''

''Let's do another circuit,'' Rafe said, handing her the binoculars.

This time they walked in silence, moving fast, looking around them for smouldering debris which could have been blown by the wind to the treed area near the camp. After a while Rafe put an arm around her waist, his fingers touching the bare skin where her T-shirt separated from her pants. The touch steadied her, and she leaned against him as they walked. What it all meant she didn't know and she didn't care—it was enough that he was there.

The wind was blowing in their direction, a bad sign. Lilly felt almost physically sick with apprehension. Convinced that the oppressive heat was at least partly from the fires, it seemed to fuel the fear that lay over the camp.

As they were returning towards the road, the second time around, they passed close to the first-aid tents, where they exchanged a few words with two of the staff who were having a quick coffee-break outside.

"Hi, guys. What's the latest?" one of them said, recognizing them as the fire-vigil patrol.

"Not good. It's a lot closer than it was this morning," Rafe said soberly.

"Hell! That means we'll be on an evacuation alert before too long," the other man said matter-of-factly. "They usually like to give us an hour if they can, to get organized before we have to ship out. We're pretty well ready, anyway."

As they walked past the entrance to the mess they saw four buses coming in from the main road, to park outside the mess.

"That looks ominous," Lilly said, shining the flash-light in front of them so that they would be readily visible. Two of the buses, of the utilitarian school-bus type, they could see, had had the seats taken out of them to make way for stretchers or wheelchairs. "We should ask the drivers what's going on."

"We're taking out some of the sick, bud," one of the drivers said. "Getting them to the airstrip. We're expecting an evacuation alert pretty soon. Are you the fire-watchers?"

"Yes."

"Well, good luck to you. You take care now. Listen out for the alert."

They continued on their way, tense and sweating, crossing the road yet again to get to the vantage point.

In what seemed like a surprisingly short time, the two hours of Lilly's shift were over. "Here's the bag and the flashlight," she said to Rafe, handing it over. "I know I'm going to have trouble sleeping, even though I'm exhausted. Maybe I'll walk with you for a bit, one more circuit."

"No, don't do that," he said. "You need to lie down, even if you can't sleep. When the alarm goes, we'll need all the energy we can muster. I'll walk you to your tent."

At the entrance to her tent they went into each others arms without any sort of premeditation. "For old times' sake, take good care of yourself," she said, her face muffled against his chest. It was by no means clear what the future held for them, if anything. There was no time to think about that. "I've forgotten what we arranged for plan B."

"Meet at the airstrip," he said.

"And plan C?"

Rafe laughed grimly. "I don't think we got around to a plan C, did we? Unless it was not to get on an aircraft without the other, unless we have to. I'll think of a good plan C, maybe, while I'm walking the beat on my own."

Inside the tent, Lilly groped her way to her bed. She had wanted to tell him that she loved him, but somehow the words had not come out. Neither had he said that he loved her. That he wanted her physically was nothing new. To be honest, she wanted him.

"Is that you, Lilly?" Ashley mumbled.

"Yes, it's me," she whispered back.

"You can put on a light," Ashley said. "We're the only two here. I'm dying to know what the fire's doing."

"I'll tell you," Lilly said, putting on her flashlight, then another dim light that was hooked up to a power source. "Oh, I'm exhausted." She sat down on the side of her camp bed, which was near Ashley's. Without mincing words, she told Ashley all that she had seen, finishing up, "I think we'll be evacuating soon. There's no way those guys can put out that fire unless we get rain, and a lot of it."

They sat in silence for a while, sipping water from bottles. The fan was going in the tent, shifting the air, so that the heat was bearable. "I'm surprised we've still got electricity and water," she added.

"I haven't been able to sleep," Ashley said. "Just dozing." Lilly noted that Ashley had not undressed, that all her gear was handy and that she had fully packed.

"At least we can put our heads down and our feet up," she said. "That helps."

After changing her T-shirt for a clean one, Lilly methodically sorted and packed her gear, which did not take long. It was good to lie down on the camp bed. "We should look out for each other," she said, "make sure we both arrive at the airstrip. But if we get separated after the airstrip, I want you to know it's been good working with you, Ash. With luck, we'll meet again at the World Aid place in Toronto.''

''Even if we have to leave here,'' Ashley said, ''we may get sent back to help when the fire has burnt itself out. Hopefully it won't destroy the whole town...do you think?'' There was fear and awe in her voice.

''I don't know, Ashley,'' Lilly said wearily. ''From what I've seen of that fire, it could eat up this camp and the whole town as well. There may be no stopping it. Thank God the area of the airstrip has been cleared of trees, otherwise we might be trapped there with nowhere to go.''

Lilly lay quietly, an arm behind her head, her eyes closed, ruminating. She had wanted to get her head sorted out, to find her priorities, and now it looked as though the circumstances they were in at the camp had started to do the job for her. Everything outside the here-and-now seemed petty. It was a luxury, she thought now, to dwell *ad nauseam* on one's mental machinations, to the exclusion of real life in the present, the pressing physical danger. It was much the same, she imagined, as being told you had a terminal disease.

When they had been dozing for about twenty minutes, they heard muffled footsteps outside, which paused at the tent flap.

''May I come in?'' a male voice called.

Lilly sat up quickly, fumbling for her flashlight and

shining it on the flap. ''Come in!'' she called out, while her heart gave a sickening leap of apprehension.

The man who entered was in uniform, from the fire-marshall's office in town. ''Sorry to break in on you like this,'' he said. ''I'm going from tent to tent, letting people know that we're on a one-hour evacuation alert.''

''Oh, heck,'' she said, swinging her legs to the ground.

Ashley, who had propped herself up on her elbows to look at the man, did the same. ''This is it, then,'' she mumbled. Her eyes were bleary with exhaustion, her hair tousled. Turning to Lilly, she added, ''This is it, girl.''

''Looks like it,'' Lilly said.

''Hang on a minute,'' the man said. ''You don't have to go anywhere right now. It means that you have to be ready to go with an hour's notice. All you have to do is have your gear packed, and it looks like you've done that already. We won't actually start the evacuation protocol until the siren goes off, in which case you go to your designated place to help get the sick out, then you wait at your mustering point until you are accounted for by the fire marshall's people who will check you out onto a vehicle. Also, you sign yourself out at your usual signing-out place, just to make sure you are accounted for at all times by anyone who wants to check on your whereabouts within the next little while. The best thing you can do right now is get a bit of rest.''

"Yes. Thank you,'' Lilly said.

When he had departed, Ashley and Lilly looked at each other. "Hell!'' Ashley said. "Maybe he's right about getting rest, but there's no way I can relax now. He must be kidding. And you've got Rafe out there.''

"He will have heard the news, and he'll maybe come in here to talk to us on his rounds,'' Lilly said. "If he doesn't, I'll go out to look for him. I'm going to rest for a bit, then get up and get some coffee and something to eat.''

"I don't suppose you really hate his guts, do you?''

"No.''

They subsided back onto the camp beds, both stiff with tension, leaving the light on. As they lay there, they were both aware of an increased wind that had sprung up. They could hear it in the trees outside, and it rattled the canvas of the tent, an eerie sound.

"That's the last thing we want,'' Ashley remarked.

Lilly knew that Rafe would come to her as soon as he had heard the news that they were on evacuation alert, so she waited for him. Although he was as mixed up, it seemed, about her as she was about him, he was a man of integrity, a kind man. Accordingly, she did not doubt that he would come.

Not long after that, he came through the flap of the tent, a tall, silent figure, reassuring to the two young women who lay there, trying to relax.

"Hey," he said, raising a hand to them as he came in, "I rather thought you'd be awake. How are you both?"

"As I think I said at least once before," Ashley said, "I'd be lying if I said I wasn't scared."

"How's the fire progressing?" Lilly asked, swinging her legs over the side of her bed. It was good to have Rafe there. His vibrant physical presence seemed to fill the whole tent.

"Well, since you and I were up on the observation point, it has definitely come closer," he said soberly. "You can hear the wind. I can see that we've got to get out. There's no alternative." He looked around the tent. "I see you're ready to go."

"Yes," she said. "Maybe Ashley and I will go to the medic tents to see if we can be of any help. I don't want to get in the way."

"You won't be in the way. They need help. Will Amos is asking about you, Ashley," Rafe said, referring to the army doctor she had been working with. "You're doing your fire-watching shift with him, right?"

"Yes," Ashley said, brightening. "I have the awful feeling that the siren may go off before we start our shift."

"He's in the mess, getting something to eat, if you want to meet up with him," Rafe said. "I get the sense that he's waiting for you."

"Really? Good idea," Ashley said, getting up quickly. "This waiting is killing me." In moments she had shouldered a bag, run a hand through her messy hair and departed through the flaps. "See you in a while," she called back to them.

Lilly and Rafe both stood up. "I'm scared," she said, putting her head against his chest. Dazed and dizzy with tiredness, she could have collapsed onto the ground in his arms.

"I think it's better if you lie down for a while," he said. "You won't be any good to anyone if you collapse. You'll be a liability. Everything's ready for evacuation. There isn't anything else we have to do until the siren actually goes off. I'll look in again on the next round of my beat, and when it's over I'll rest here on Ashley's bed, to be with you. OK?"

"OK," she agreed. "Thanks." They would both feel happier knowing where the other one was. "You won't get any rest, by the sound of it."

"I'm resigned to that." He reached forward quickly and cupped her cheek with his hand. "Take care."

When he had gone she stood there feeling very much alone. Tears filled her eyes. Sleep was out of the question. Now she had something definite to focus on, she would wait until Rafe came back, then they would go to the medic tents to make themselves useful until the siren went off. If by some miracle, the fire was diverted by the wind away from Crater Lake, they could maybe hang on longer, after airlifting their patients out. Somehow she did not think that would be the case.

Running footsteps impinged on her consciousness some time later, and she sat up as Rafe came through the tent flap. By his sense of urgency, she could tell that their tentative plans had changed. He strode over to her and squatted down by her bed.

"A change of plan," he said breathlessly. "Ashley and Will Amos are starting their fire-watching shift early because I have to accompany a couple of seriously injured guys to the airstrip right now to see them on a plane. If the siren goes off here soon, I may not come back here, in which case I'll meet you at the airstrip. It will depend on how much time I have."

"I see," she said, nodding, trying not to let him see that she would feel bereft without him in the camp.

"We have to scuttle our plan A, to meet at the mustering point, and go directly to plan B—meet at the airstrip," he said with a rueful grin.

"Thank God for plan B," she said jokingly, trying to make light of what was becoming more and more a run-up to zero hour. "Take good care of yourself, Rafe." They hugged each other. The gesture came spontaneously.

"I will. And you do the same. Don't take any risks whatsoever. Promise?"

"I promise," she said.

"Stick to the protocol, that's the best thing," he said emphatically. "The guys here know what they're doing. Go and join up with Will and Ashley right now. That's the best thing. Don't stay here on your own."

"All right," she agreed.

"Gotta go." With a last squeeze to her arms, he let go and moved away from her, leaving her with an intense sensation of feeling utterly bereft.

Then he was gone, his footsteps receding quickly into the night. Lilly sat on the bed, tears running down her face. The tent was a lonely place, bathed in the dim green light, the soughing of the wind outside bringing disaster with it. She sat with her elbows propped on her knees, her face in her hands. If anything positive came out of this trip, it was most likely that she would have her private life sorted out…at least in her head. Rafe's kindness did not mean that he had given up his bitterness where she was concerned.

There were things to do. After filling two water bottles and stowing them in her rucksack, she washed her face and hands, brushed her teeth, ran a brush through her hair, folded up her camp bed and put her gear together in a neat pile. Now she was ready to go over to the medic tents to offer her services, after she had got herself a snack and coffee.

# CHAPTER SIX

''Am I glad to see you,'' John said to Lilly when she entered the tent where she had been working earlier. From his appearance she could tell that he had not even tried to get any sleep. Terry was there, too, rushing about. ''We've already shipped out the more serious of our cases and we've decided to get the rest out before the siren goes. We're just waiting for more vehicles. One or two of the guys who were here have rejoined the firefighting crews…the ones who were only a bit dehydrated.''

''What do you want me to do?''

''Match these charts here to the patients, then take patient and chart, with a wheelchair or stretcher, out to the buses at the entrance to the mess,'' he said.

Lilly picked up a chart from a row that John had set out neatly on a makeshift table. ''I see that Alec Ingram's still here,'' she said. ''I'll take him first, shall I?''

''Yeah. We're a bit worried about him because he's still not passing as much urine as he should, even though he's on a diuretic,'' John said. ''Take that wheelchair over there, the one with the IV pole on it.''

''OK.''

All the men in the main body of the tent were awake, which was not surprising with all the comings and goings, the noise, as well as the increasing urgency to get out that pervaded the place.

"Hello, Alec," Lilly said, pushing the chair up to his camp bed. "I've come to take you to the transport for the airstrip."

"Hi," he said. "Don't you people ever sleep?"

"No, not here," she said, smiling at him. It was good to be doing something. Focusing on work, she did not dwell too much on the massive fire that was roaring in the forest not too far away from them, or that Rafe was on his way to the airstrip. "How are you?"

"Not normal, that's for sure," he said. "But not too bad either."

"We'll get you to a proper hospital," she said, lifting his intravenous fluid bag from the metal pole behind his bed and putting it on the pole attached to the wheelchair. "I'm taking you out to one of the buses."

"I'm relieved to be going," he said. "If I can't fight fires here, I may as well be out of it."

She pushed him out into the warm, humid night, going towards a lighted bus that was parked outside the mess door. Just as they came up, another bus came off the main road and drove up to park near the other one.

A soldier with a clipboard took Alec's chart from Lilly and wrote the name down on a sheet of paper.

The bus had a lifting device that took the wheelchair into the body of the bus, where Lilly helped her patient transfer to a special comfortable seat that could be tilted to the horizontal position.

When he was settled, they shook hands. "Good luck," she said. "You'll soon be out of here."

"Thanks a million," he said. "Good luck to you, too."

As Lilly went down the steps of the bus, taking the wheelchair with her, she considered that maybe she needed to be wished luck more than he did. While he was getting out, she would be one of the last to leave.

Several times she made the trip, moving quickly, until the first bus was full. As she stood there, watching it leave the community centre parking lot and turn onto the main road, she felt a touch on her arm.

"Hey, Lilly," Ashley said at her elbow. "How goes it?"

"Hi." She turned to smile at Ashley and Will. Will was a tall, muscular, good-looking man, rather quiet, who was clearly attracted to Ashley. On the few occasions that Lilly had spoken to him, he'd seemed like a very nice, genuine man, with a witty, dry sense of humour.

"What do the fires look like from up on the vantage point?" she enquired.

"Not good," Will said. "You're doing the right thing in getting these men out now."

"See you. Take care," Ashley said, waving as she

and her companion disappeared into the darker regions of the camp.

Impulsively, Lilly ran to the entrance of the mess and went in to look at the sign-in book to see if, by any chance, Rafe had returned to camp, even though she suspected that he would not have had time to get to the airstrip and back. No, he had not signed in. What that meant, she was not sure. Maybe it meant that there was not an aircraft ready to take the men out, that he could not leave his patients. There would be a reasonable explanation, yet the sight of his signature and name as having signed out left her with a feeling of apprehension and loss.

Although they had agreed to meet at the airstrip, she knew he would try to return to the camp if he had time to do so before all the other patients were evacuated, thinking he might be needed. No doubt there would be other firefighters who needed medical attention. There would be a contingency plan to set up a first-aid post somewhere else, maybe at the other end of the town, closer to the airstrip and safety.

Running, she went back to the tent. The second bus was now being loaded up. It was a slow business as they had to make each patient safe and secure within the vehicle.

''When we've got the patients in, Lilly,'' John said to her, ''we can get some of our equipment into trucks, but not all, of course, because we have to stay open for business. Only when the siren goes off do we get it all in, and the guys can come in to take down the tents.''

"John," she said tensely, "are we going to set up a post somewhere else? There must be more people in need of medical help.''

"Yep," he said. "I believe it's going to be at the main marina in town, where there's a metal boathouse. That will be the last stand here, so to speak. Someone will confirm that before we shift out of here. Then we can set up shop again at the airstrip, pretty quickly, if we have to.''

"Do you know where Jessie is?'' she asked. "I haven't
seen her for a while.''

"Yep," he said. "I know where she is at all times. She's OK, don't you worry." Impulsively, he gave her a quick, awkward hug. "Don't you worry now, everything's under control. The only thing that isn't under control is the bloody fire. But we're going to be at least two steps ahead of that. OK?''

"OK, John," she said, smiling. "Thanks for keeping my spirits up. I'm new to this game. If I don't get a chance to say this again, it's been great working with you…if only for two days.''

"Ditto," he said. "Sometimes two days can seem like two weeks. And in case you didn't know, 'cheerful' is my middle name. My third name is 'realism'. With that, you can't go wrong in this game.''

Back and forth she went, back and forth, moving

people and boxes of equipment, everything carefully labelled so that they would know exactly where everything was when they had to set up again.

Although they were all expecting the siren, it was a shock when it actually went off with a loud, high-pitched wail that could no doubt be heard for miles around. Many of the personnel there had never before heard such a siren, and it triggered a feeling of dread.

Lilly jumped nervously as she packed IV bags of fluid into a large, clear plastic carton, exchanging meaningful glances with John who was doing the same thing. ''This is it,'' he said. ''No more speculation, no more messing about.''

Terry came running into the prep area. ''Thank God we got all our patients out,'' he said. ''What now?''

''Get the trolley,'' John said urgently, his voice raised above the wail of the siren. ''Get all this gear loaded, pronto.''

They all turned quickly as Jessie came in through the door, sporting a slight limp, in her usual state of dishevelment. ''You OK, John? Everything under control?'' she said. ''Terry? Lilly?''

''Everything's just dandy,'' John said. ''The better for seeing you, little darling. I was wondering where the hell you were.''

''I'm all right,'' she said. Then, no doubt against army regulations, they hugged each other and kissed. ''Pack up and get the hell out.''

''And you?'' John said tensely.

"I have a few more things to do," she said calmly. "Then I'm going to get the hell out, too."

"Keep me informed," John said, tension behind his casual words.

"I will, John," she said, going out, blowing him a kiss as she went. "You take care, now."

After she had gone, the three of them pushed their boxed equipment out to a truck. Lilly was panting with the effort in the warm climate, sweat pouring from her body. At the same time, she could see the cooks and kitchen staff from the mess loading up their gear also. Very soon the whole camp would be packed up and ready to go, then it would become a sort of ghost town until the remaining firefighters retreated from where they were now, closer to the community, fighting the fire as they came. If something did not happen to give them a break, it would roar into Crater Lake and consume it.

"Don't think about that," Lilly muttered to herself as she ran back to the tent to get another load. She could see Ashley and Will doing the same from the next medic tent, having given up their fire-watching job momentarily.

When all was packed and the crews moved in to take down the tents, Lilly ran back to the mess to check the book again, hoping that in the controlled chaos of the evacuating camp, she might have missed Rafe's return. There was a small line of people checking out. While she was there, she would sign herself out. The last person in authority in the camp would take the book.

No, he was not there; she checked quickly before signing out herself. Stifling a feeling of dread, she hurried back, trying not to read too much into his absence, telling herself that he was safe and sound at the airstrip.

More buses had arrived and people were getting on them now, having their names checked off by a worker from the fire-marshall's department.

John was outside one of the medic tents. ''Run and get your gear, Lilly,'' he said. ''Make it snappy. Ashley was just here asking for you. She's gone over there to your tent.''

''Thanks.'' Running, she headed towards their tent. The air now was acrid with a denser smoke.

Ashley was in the tent, shouldering her bags. ''Thank God it's you,'' she said. ''I was getting worried. Any sign of Rafe?''

''No.''

It took seconds only to shoulder her rucksack, to take a bag in either hand. In moments they were hurrying back along the path in the darkness towards the buses. ''Oh, Rafe, Rafe.'' She said his name over and over again to herself. ''Where are you?''

Her relief at being able to get on a bus, to have her name and ID badge checked by the officer in charge of the evacuation, was tempered by her anxiety about Rafe. ''Is Dr Rafe Neilson on your list?'' she asked.

"He's one of the doctors with World Aid. He went to the airstrip with patients earlier. I thought maybe he had come back."

Swiftly the officer checked the list, which was in alphabetical order. "No, he's not here," he said. "Most likely he's been detained at the airstrip. It's a bit chaotic there. He'll be more useful there, he wouldn't have any reason to come back here."

Except for me, Lilly said to herself as she got onto the bus and found herself a seat next to Ashley. John, Terry and Will got on last.

As the bus moved away from the community centre up onto the main road, Ashley twisted around in her seat to look behind them, up the road. "Look at that," she whispered to Lilly.

All the people on the bus turned. There was a red glow in the sky above the nearer trees, and they could see the flames shooting up into the black night sky on a wide front, the trees unaffected as yet forming a fragile barrier between them and the voracious flames.

"Hell!" someone said. The rest remained silent. Lilly clutched her rucksack to her on her lap, as though the guarding of her few very personal possessions in that bag, a talisman, would keep her safe. As the bus gained speed, she thought of her parents, no doubt hearing about the fires on the radio news, maybe seeing it on television, and she had a stab of intense remorse that she had not yet telephoned them. Cosy, safe

Albertstown, together with her family, seemed infinitely dear at that moment.

"Rafe...where are you?" she whispered.

After that quick look towards the fires, after those first exclamations of shock, no one looked back but concentrated on the road ahead that was illuminated by the comforting, benign yellow glow of the headlights. There was no chatter. It appeared that people had been shocked into silence, together with their fatigue.

Lilly found herself willing the bus to move faster, away from the danger, towards where she hoped Rafe would be. From the windows they could see men in the main street of Crater Lake hosing down buildings with water. There were a few vehicles coming and going. Some small boats were tied up to the wooden jetties that projected out into the lake, while more of the motorboats had been taken out to a safer place in the lake. As they moved, Lilly wondered whether she and Ashley and Rafe would be coming back to Crater Lake, whether there would be anything left to come back to.

Near the end of the town, before they entered the darkness of the road to the airstrip, someone flagged down the bus and it came to a halt. Jessie got on, with her rucksack and bag.

"Hey, Jess!" a few people called to her.

"Hey," she said, looking around for John, who had kept a seat for her beside him. Lilly could tell that

John was immensely relieved to see her. They sat holding hands as the bus started up again.

Rafe, where are you? She said the words to herself, despairingly.

The road to the airstrip took them through areas that were wooded, in danger of catching fire. Someone had told her that there was at least one other alternative route to the airstrip, so that they would not be entirely cut off in the town, and that there was a small road out of the community, through a forest, to the next small town many miles away. From that small town, there was no road out.

"Have you called your family since you've been here?" Ashley asked her. The two of them were sitting together, with Will behind.

"No. Things have been so hectic," she admitted. "I feel bad about it, because they must be pretty worried. I thought I'd do it at the airstrip, if we can find a pay-phone, now I know what we're doing. I didn't want to alarm them before. My mother always knows when I'm not telling the absolute truth."

"Same here," Ashley said.

"I'm worried about Rafe," Lilly said. "I checked the sign-in book, he hadn't come back to camp."

"He'll be at the airstrip," Ashley said. "Where else would he be?"

Lilly shrugged, her anxiety feeling like a physical weight on her shoulders. "We have a plan to meet there,'' she said. ''I don't know what I'll do if he's not there.''

''Deal with that when, or if, it happens,'' Ashley said. ''Will said that he will be setting up a first-aid post at the airstrip, so he won't get out until he has to. I might just stay with him...if he'll let me.''

''That sounds like a good idea,'' Lilly said. ''I think he'll be glad to have you.''

There seemed to be a collective sigh and lightening of the atmosphere when the bus pulled in to the driveway to the airstrip. They could see planes and one helicopter on the tarmac, buses and other vehicles beside them, unloading personnel and equipment. It looked chaotic, with all the comings and goings, like a scene from a film, part in light, part in semi-darkness.

The driver of their bus, a soldier, took them away from the main entrance to park in a quiet spot of a spacious parking lot, then he rose from his seat to address them. ''Check in, give your name to the guy just to the left of the entrance when you get inside. You'll see a sign for volunteers, separate from army personnel and the sick and injured. You'll be checked out when you get on a plane. Please don't leave the building. We have to know where you are at all times.''

''Thank you,'' they chorused, subdued yet relieved. Soon they would be out of it.

They straggled across with their bags to the entrance, to join the milling crowd there. Although it had looked uncoordinated from a distance, all was orderly and controlled, they could see close up.

Lilly got in line to give her name. "Lilly Page, with World Aid, a volunteer," she said. "I'm concerned about a colleague of mine, Dr Rafe Neilson. He left the camp to come here with some of the injured, and he didn't check back in again. Is he here?"

"Just a second." The soldier riffled through some papers. "Dr Neilson...yes, he was here. He left here to go back to Crater Lake, over an hour ago."

"What? But he didn't get there," she said. "At least, not to the army camp."

"Hang on. It says here he left a note for you. Lilly Page, right?"

"Yes." Her heart was thudding with fear. If he had gone back, why had they not seen him? They had not passed any vehicles on the road going back.

"It's right here on my clipboard," the soldier said, handing her a folded sheet of paper. "I remember him. He got a ride back to town in an ambulance."

"Thanks."

Ashley, who had been standing next to her, took her arm. "Let's get something to eat and drink," she said. "We don't know when we might get another opportunity. You've gone as white as a sheet." After she had given her own name, Ashley guided her out of the line.

"I'm all right. I just want to read this."

"Come on, there's a booth over there. We can sit down."

Following Ashley, in something of a daze, with the crumpled note in her hand, Lilly soon found herself sitting with a paper cup of coffee in her hand. Wanting to look at the note, yet reluctant, she sipped coffee.

"This was our plan B," she said to Ashley. "We don't have a plan C."

Ashley stared at her. "Try not to worry, Lilly," she said. "Rafe can look after himself, from what I've seen of him."

The note said that Rafe had gone back to Crater Lake, getting a ride with a civilian ambulance, because there had been a series of accidents at the main boat-house at the main jetty and he had gone to help. A first-aid post was to be set up there anyway, so he had been informed. He would either meet her at the airstrip, or at the next town, he said. She was to get on a plane and not wait for him.

Silently she handed the note to Ashley to read, while she compressed her lips together to prevent them from trembling as tears pricked her eyes. This scenario was just what she had wanted to avoid.

"He'll be all right," Ashley said. "He knows what he's doing."

"He's a doctor," Lilly said. "Not a firefighter."

"He's used to emergency situations," Ashley persisted. "You don't have to play mother, Lilly."

"Lover," she said. "I'm his lover. To the ends of the earth…"

"This place could be the end of the earth."

Lilly took a swallow of coffee as her eyes played over the crowd before them, seeing the urgent yet controlled comings and going of the people being evacuated. "I'm going back to Crater Lake," she said evenly, making up her mind in the instance the words came out of her mouth. "Cover for me, Ashley. Tell them I've gone, but only after I've gone. Can you take my bags on the plane with you, please? I'll just keep my rucksack with me."

"You can't do that!" Ashley said, gripping her arm again, putting her face squarely in front of Lilly's face. "They won't let you out of here. And even if they did, how would you get back there, then back here? It's madness. You could be trapped by fire. Someone's just gone to a hell of a lot of trouble to get us out."

"I know," she said. "I must go, Ashley. There's no way I could get on a plane out of here without Rafe." Having said those words, a strange, cool feeling of calm came over her. "I love him, you see, and without him my life doesn't have much meaning."

"Maybe so. But one of the things they are trying to teach us at World Aid is not to behave rashly in times of crisis. And going back to a fire, which will be right in Crater Lake itself before too long, is acting rashly, Lilly," Ashley said.

"It's a calculated risk, Ashley, that I've decided to

take,'' she said. ''If anything. Rafe will need my help. There's a civilian ambulance driver over there, bringing in someone on a stretcher. I'll get a ride back with him, as I expect he's going back there.''

''He'd be mad to take you,'' Ashley said.

''We'll see.'' She gave Ashley a quick, fierce hug. ''Cover for me, Ash. Thanks.''

Shouldering her rucksack quickly, leaving her other two bags at Ashley's feet, she stood up and strode away.

''Wait! Lilly!'' Ashley's urgent voice called behind her, but she did not turn.

After a quick detour into a women's washroom— where she stared at herself uncomprehendingly in the mirror on the way out again, not recognizing the wild-eyed, sweat-stained young woman with the tufty hair who stared back at her—she made her way by a slightly circuitous route back to the main entrance where she had seen the ambulance driver.

The soldier with the clipboard stared at her, so she made a motion as though she were smoking a cigarette and wanted to go outside to do it, so he gave a nod. Feeling calm, yet very keyed up at the same time, rather as she always felt before a major operation in the operating room of a hospital, she pushed her way through the double glass doors into the humid night and the general comings and goings.

Soon the ambulance driver would come back out again. Over to her left she could see one ambulance parked, which must be the one that he had come in. Having already formulated a plan, she would get a ride back into town with him. Yes, it was madness, but calculated, she told herself. There was no way she could leave without at least knowing exactly where Rafe was. If they saw another vehicle on the road, maybe they could stop and find out if he was on it.

Feeling conspicuous, she stood behind the ambulance in relative darkness, peeping out from time to time. In due course, the driver came out, pushing the stretcher on wheels.

"Hello," she accosted him. "Could you give me a ride back to Crater Lake, to the main boathouse at the jetty? I'm with World Aid and I've been ordered to meet up with Dr Rafe Neilson there, to help him." She handed him her laminated ID badge. "I'm Lilly Page, RN. I've been checked out." While she regretted the lie, she had the sense that he would not take her otherwise.

He looked at her dubiously, then down at her ID. "I can give you a ride," he said. "But it sure isn't safe there any more. I would have to know where you were to get you out again if I had to. I was the one who took Dr Neilson back. I don't know how many vehicles will be left there to get you back here."

"Dr Neilson will have arranged transport," she said calmly. "Maybe if we see a vehicle coming this way we could flag it down and see if he's on it. I...I've arranged to rendezvous with him at the boathouse."

Only when the ambulance left the driveway of the airstrip to turn into the darkness of the main road back to Crater Lake did the full impact of her action come home to her. Once safe at the airstrip, with planes waiting, it had indeed been madness to leave. She could have simply waited there for Rafe, not got on a plane. But she knew that by doing this she was being true to herself, true to him. In a very odd sort of way everything seemed to be coming together, and that in itself brought a peace of sorts. Indeed, it seemed that someone else was making the decisions for her, another, calmer self, who was telling her what to do.

They drove in silence as the road twisted. Both were very conscious that the fire could spread to the trees there, which crowded the road densely. As they got closer to Crater Lake, they could see the glow of fire in the sky, high above the trees.

Smoke was dense as they came into Crater Lake, at the other end from the community centre. There were fire trucks in the main street, with firefighters hosing down buildings under a pall of smoke.

''I'm going to be parking this vehicle by the main boathouse for now, until I have patients to take back to the airstrip.'' the driver said. ''Keep in touch with me so that I can get you out if I have to. In an emergency, if we get ringed by fire, you can take a small rowing boat out onto the lake and wait it out...one of the aluminum ones, not the motorboats, which have tanks full of gas, most likely. There will be a few pick-up trucks and vans here still.''

''Thanks for telling me, and for the ride.''

''Why don't you run in,'' he said, ''and see if Dr Neilson's there? They've made this into a first-aid post. If he's not there, it might be wiser for you to get the hell out of here, on another vehicle going back to the airstrip or with me. Let me know quickly. I have to pick up a couple of guys at another first-aid post, then I'll be back here.''

''All right,'' Lilly said as she jumped out of the ambulance, but with no intention of going back to the airstrip without Rafe. From what she could see, by looking around her quickly, the boathouse was more of a clubhouse, with an adjacent large repair workshop for boats, than an actual boathouse, as it was several hundred yards back from the lake.

Inside the large boathouse, made from metal posts and metal siding, she could see that a temporary first-aid post had been set up, no doubt with some of the equipment from the community centre. Lilly stood just inside the door, casting her eyes around quickly. Then she saw Rafe, bending over a man on a makeshift examination table, splinting a leg. The relief that she felt was like a dead weight being lifted from her shoulders, and she knew she had done the right thing in coming back. The knowledge gave her a sense of peace, of quiet confidence.

When he saw her his face stiffened with shock, then,

with a few words to the man he was working on, he strode over to Lilly. He looked more exhausted than she had ever seen him, his face unshaven and drawn, unnaturally pale. He would be running on adrenaline, as they all were.

"What the hell are you doing here? You should be out of here," he said, incredulous. "I was going on the assumption that you were safe." He sounded angry, exasperated. "Don't you realize that this whole place is about to go up in flames?"

"That's the second time you've asked me that," she said, so relieved to see him that she didn't care what mood he was in, what he thought of her. "Yes, I do know what's going on here. We agreed to meet at the airstrip. Plan B, remember? I could ask you the same question. What the hell are you doing here?"

"There's work for me here, I had to come back," he said, staring at her with glazed eyes in his haggard face. "The other doctors are either at the airstrip or in the town at another first-aid post. They need me here. I suggest you get on the first ambulance out of here. The last thing I need is to be worried about you."

Lilly stared back at him defiantly. "No! I'm not getting out. There's no way I can leave here without you. You don't know me at all if you think I could. I would be worried sick. That's the last thing I need."

"That wasn't the impression I got over the past few weeks, Lilly," he said tiredly, keeping his voice low so that the men he was treating could not hear. ''No matter. We're needed here.''

Lilly chose not to respond to that first remark. ''I must speak to the ambulance driver,'' she said decisively. ''Then I'm going to take a quick look at the jetty. We may have to make our escape that way, by boat.''

Before he could say anything else, she turned quickly and went out. ''He's there!'' she called to the ambulance driver, who had the engine running. ''Everything's fine! I'm staying.''

When he had driven away, she ran down towards the jetty, down a narrow, deserted street where, surprisingly, electric streetlamps were still lit. Any time now those would be going out, she speculated. At the end of the road there was a wide, substantial jetty, going quite a long way out into the water, made of wood.

Lilly, out of breath now, walked fast along its length. There were several rowing boats tied up there at the very end, with oars and life-jackets in the bilges. Only one motorboat remained, on the opposite side of the jetty. With a tank full of fuel, it would be like a bomb waiting to go off when the fire got to the jetty. No doubt someone would have removed it to the centre of the lake by then, she thought, taking a good look around her, trying to imprint everything on her mind so that if they had to run through dense smoke, she would know where to go. Perhaps there would be no need; perhaps they would all be on their way to the airstrip by then.

Satisfied that she would remember, even if they had little light, she turned and ran back up the incline to the boathouse. Looking in the direction of the community centre, she saw an ominous red glow in the sky.

"What can I do?" she said breathlessly to Rafe as he bent over a man, putting a temporary cast on a leg.

"See to those two guys," he said curtly, gesturing to two men who were lying on wooden tables that had been commandeered as treatment tables. "All the supplies we have are in these plastic cartons next to the sink over there. We need to get a move on. We may lose our electricity very soon, and I want all these guys ready for departure when the ambulance driver comes back. There's Demerol for pain, as well as some local anaesthetic."

"Right," she said.

In moments she had assessed the situation, put on a plastic apron over her less than clean clothes, washed her hands in the kitchen area and was cleaning serious wounds on two firefighters, having injected the affected areas with local anaesthetic. Some of those wounds needed to be sutured, but for now she would clean and irrigate them, then put on butterfly sutures to hold the edges of the wounds together. There were preloaded syringes for anti-tetanus shots. They also had to guard against gas gengrene in wounds that had been exposed to dirt, particularly puncture wounds where oxygen could not penetrate easily.

All this went through her mind with lightning speed as she worked. The odd sense of peace remained with her, knowing that Rafe was a mere few feet away from her, as she kept her head bent to her work. There was no need to talk. She could see what had to be done, and the equipment that they had to work with was in evidence. The sense of urgency pervaded the room like an electric current as the injured men rested in sheer exhaustion, eyes closed, and stoically submitted themselves to what had to be done. There was an atmosphere of suppressed tension and fear held in check.

Only tentatively did she let her mind wander to the fires close by. They would get some warning, she and Rafe and the men, if they had to get out in a hurry. The army knew they were there.

Momentarily she stood beside Rafe at the sink as they both put used instruments in a metal dish to soak in antiseptic. "There's a van parked outside," he said to her tersely, "to the left of the building, with the key in the ignition. That's our escape vehicle when we have to leave. I'm hoping these men will have gone in the ambulance before we have to get out, but anything is possible. We may have to make a run for it with them."

"All right," she said.

"This is an ice box," he said, putting his hand on

a large plastic container. "There's food and water in it. We'll put the whole thing in the van when we finally get out."

When she had come in, there had been one hurricane lantern burning, fuelled by kerosene. Now Rafe lit two more.

Back at work, she spoke quietly to the man she was working on, keeping conversation to a minimum. Each man had an identity form with a very brief history of his injuries hastily scrawled on it. "You'll soon be out of here," she said.

He had a blood-soaked bandage on one arm and another around his head. "Yeah," he said. "Call me Kev."

"I'm Lilly Page." All head injuries had to be taken very seriously. "When you get to a hospital, you'll need a skull X-ray as soon as possible. Ask for one, if it isn't immediately forthcoming."

He nodded, resigned and relieved. "Yeah, I will," he said wearily. "Thanks. Great to meet you. I reckon I'll be out of here."

"Looks like it," she said.

When she glanced at Rafe he smiled, to her surprise, and gave her the thumbs-up sign. Perhaps he could tell that she was nervous about dealing with this head injury. With a pair of scissors she cut off the soiled dressings on her patient and set to work. There was a gash on his forehead, about four inches long, down to the bone, dark red with congealed blood.

Even without a skull X-ray, she could check her patient for signs and symptoms of bleeding inside the skull, which could be very serious.

In spite of the fear, the danger, it was good to be doing what she had come here to do, to use her training and experience in this way. It was even better to have the man she loved doing the same thing just a few feet away from her, and she found her eyes straying to him now and again to make sure he was really there. More often than not, he was looking back at her. For a long time she had not felt so alive.

"Did you really think I would leave here without you?" she asked quietly while again she washed the instruments she had used at the sink, while he did the same.

"To be honest, Lilly, I wasn't absolutely sure," he said, also keeping his voice down. "I wanted to get you out of here."

Had she not told him recently that she loved him? Or had she only thought it? There had been a time when she had said it.

The tension between them was not now a negative tension in any way. It was more a positive, intense awareness and seemed to hold possibilities in it. Perhaps, after all, the best parts of the past could be held on to. If only he felt that way, too.

"Assuming we'll get out of this boathouse OK," he said. "Our plan C now is that we'll stay close."

"One of the paramedics said to take a rowing boat

out into the lake if the fire gets to us here," she said. "If we can't get a vehicle out to the airstrip, that is."

"That's the general plan. Great idea," he said, "if we can get down to the water. The other escape route is a vehicle along the road, as you say."

Twenty minutes later, just as Lilly had more or less finished a final dressing, the electric lights went out, leaving them in the dim light of the kerosene lamps. "Just what we need," one of the men joked.

"At least we've still got water," someone else said.

"Knock on wood."

"We're just about finished here, so it doesn't matter," Rafe said, loud enough that everyone could hear. "Any minute now, at least one ambulance should be here to take you out."

All the suitable receptacles on hand had been filled with water, Lilly noted. Everyone there had at least two filled water bottles for drinking purposes.

As though on cue, two ambulances arrived at the same time to get the men. When the last of the injured men had been taken out, Lilly and Rafe knew that their job was done at the boathouse. As the remaining people retreated from Crater Lake, the injured would go to the airstrip for first aid.

In the light of the kerosene lamps, they quickly began to pack up what was left of the equipment, although a lot of it had gone already in the last truck. Lilly used spaghetti tongs to lift the last of the sterilized instruments out of the large pot in which they had been boiling on a propane stove. She ran cold water over them, dried them and packed them away in a box. Other equipment and supplies—medications, local anaesthetics, hypodermic syringes and needles, and dressings—was all efficiently packed in the appropriate boxes. They would carry these out to their escape van.

"We'll take the kerosene lamps with us," Rafe said "We don't want to add fuel to the flames if this place catches fire."

As though on another cue, the door opened noisily and a firefighter came in. "Better get out, you guys," he said. "Fast."

"What's up?" Rafe said.

"Some of the buildings are on fire in the main street, near the other end, and the wind's blowing burning debris over in this direction. There's a stiff wind. Just what we need, eh?" the firefighter said ruefully.

"Will it get this far?"

"With a wind like that, you betcha! I see you've got a van out there." He paused to look around the boathouse. "Take anything flammable with you. Let me have your names, so that I know you've been accounted for."

"Right."

"Lock the place up, so that we don't get anyone else taking shelter here, or setting up shop of some sort," the firefighter said with grim humour, "although I don't suppose there's much chance of that. This place is metal, it would be like an oven.''

When he had gone, Lilly and Rafe carried the remaining boxes out to the van, moving quickly, careful to take the remaining food and water.

''Get into the van, Lilly,'' Rafe said as they stood together in the street. ''I'll go back in to get the kerosene lamps and then I'll lock up.'' They could hear the roar of fire and the glow of it lit up the street. Not in her wildest imaginings had she thought that they would be this close to it. Her throat felt tight with fear, her heart thudding.

''Hurry,'' she said, as she pushed the last two boxes into the back of the van and slammed the door.

There was a brilliant glow from fires around them, just out of sight, so that she felt a sense of sick excitement as she looked around her. It was terrifying how quickly fire had spread to the buildings of the main street by gobbets of burning wood blown long distances by the wind. Even so, she did not doubt that they would get out safely.

Quite suddenly, two chunks of burning debris came down near her on the road. As she stared at them in amazement, she looked up and saw more pieces higher up above the buildings which seemed to float there before spiralling down slowly towards her, as though they were in a macabre dance. ''Hey! Rafe, hurry up!'' she shouted, as she saw him coming out of the boat-house then turning to lock the door. In one hand he carried four kerosene lanterns, their flames extinguished.

"Hell!" he said, as more chunks of burning debris floated down. "Those are bits of asphalt, by the look of them, from the roofs up the street. Get into the van."

As he stowed the lanterns on the floor of the van by the rear seats, two large pieces of flaming debris landed close to the van, burning vigorously on the ground.

"Oh, God!" Lilly said, casting around quickly for something to use to move them away. The last thing they needed was for the van to catch fire.

Against the side of the boathouse someone had left a set of short oars. Using one of them, she flung the burning debris away into the centre of the road, then shifted it to the other side. Looking up, she saw other chunks of burning material floating down on top of the building opposite the boathouse, where it continued to burn. Sparks were shooting up and chunks were falling like huge, red, obscene snowflakes, coming out of a black sky that was tinged with red at its base.

For the first time Lilly felt her fear turning to something like terror. All she knew then was that she had never before felt such immediate fear for her own physical safety and that of the man she loved. In seconds, her confidence that they would get out unscathed had shifted to less of a certainty.

She remembered then what the firefighter had said

at the orientation talk in the mess hall: a stiff wind could blow burning debris as far as two kilometres. The boathouse and the buildings opposite and around it were much closer than two kilometres from other burning buildings. The fire was leapfrogging its way towards them.

Thick and fast, the pieces began to fall around her as she opened the passenger door to get in. "That building is on fire!" she screamed to Rafe, pointing up to the building opposite. They could see that the roof was on fire, could hear the crackling noise that it made. All around them the air had filled with smoke and the stench of burning materials.

"Come on," Rafe shouted, taking her arm. "Get in."

Just then, a chunk of burning material landed right on Rafe's shoulder and Lilly screamed. Quickly he brushed it off, but his shirt was on fire. Lilly rushed forward and beat at the flames with her hands.

"Stand back!" he shouted, as he ripped his shirt off over his head and flung it from him. He shoved her into the van, slammed the door and ran round to the driver's side, while they quickly became surrounded by fires burning in the road.

The heat had increased very noticeably in the last few minutes and they watched, horrified, as the burning roof before them collapsed with a roar into the interior of the building.

"It didn't take much for that to go," Rafe said, with grim understatement.

Rafe got the engine started and eased the van out further into the road. If they could make a sharp left turn, they could maybe just make it up to the main road to the airstrip.

Rafe's naked torso gleamed with sweat, red in patches where the flames had touched him. Before he could make the turn, there was the loud roar of an explosion and the burning building opposite erupted into a huge ball of fire, reaching over towards them. The roar of it was like a tank coming at them. In seconds, their escape route from the small side street into the main street had been cut off.

Lilly heard someone screaming and realized that the sound was coming from her own mouth.

"Hang on tight!" Rafe yelled, his hands gripping the steering-wheel as though he feared it would leap out of his grasp. "I'm going to make a run for it down to the jetty."

Hanging on grimly to either side of her seat, Lilly began to pray. She knew that it was not a good idea to go towards a fire, into a fire. Right now, the main street was most likely blocked. The speed with which the fire was moving had been previously unimaginable.

With great skill, Rafe manoeuvred the small van round in the tightest possible space, until it was facing the direction of the jetty. There was a wall of flame both behind and in front of them now. They both made an educated, silent guess that the wall was less dense in the direction of the jetty. The vehicle was not a safe place, with a tank full of gas, but neither would they be safe on foot. They had no alternative but to brazen it out, to make a frantic dash for it.

Rafe gunned the engine. "Get down!" he yelled. "Get down!"

Lilly screamed. Trying to make herself as small as possible, she put her head down on her knees. Thank God they were together…thank God! That was all she could think of in the seconds it took for the car to rush forward. If they were to die, she wanted to be with Rafe.

The van jerked forward, rushing through the wall of flame. She could not look. The heat, the noise, the redness of it snatched at them as though to devour them. It was all impersonal and powerful; there was nothing they could do other than what they were doing now, hoping to outrun it.

Suddenly they were through the other side, rushing down the illuminated road, garish in the red glow, like the inferno of hell. Lilly looked up. By some miracle the van was not on fire, the headlights still worked, the engine still worked. They had taken an enormous risk, because there had been no alternative.

The jetty seemed to be rushing towards them through billowing black and grey smoke. There was no reality for Lilly, except the fight for life, for herself, for Rafe whom she loved. Intense fear made you live in the moment, she knew that now. Her whole body was tense, her mind hyper-alert, like that of an animal that had been cornered by a predator and knew that it must turn and fight for its life.

She and Rafe were attuned to each other in moments of intense concentration. They were both trained, in their various ways, for emergencies. Now they were fighting for themselves, concentrating because their lives depended on it.

Fearlessly, it seemed to her, Rafe drove the van fast down the remaining stretch of road and onto the wooden jetty, to near the far end, and brought it to a stop. When the engine was switched off, bringing a comparative silence, they sat in shock, panting for breath.

Then Rafe turned his head to look at her in the red glow that now illuminated the jetty, all electric light having gone. ''All right?'' he said.

''Yes,'' she whispered, ''all right.''

''Listen,'' he said. ''We're going to go to one of those metal rowing boats, put on life-jackets, row out a bit, then turn right from there up the shoreline in the direction of the airstrip. We won't go out to the centre of the lake, because there are a lot of other boats out there. About a mile along the shore, there's a small jetty. We'll tie up there and rest for a while, have something to eat, stay near the boat in case we get cut off by fire again. There's a path out of there to the main road, so I've been told. We won't hang about in the woods.''

"Yes, OK." Lilly's voice came out in a croak. "It sounds good.''

Deliberately Lilly did not look back at the fire which they could hear roaring behind them as they selected a rowing boat, put their rucksacks and the box of food and water in it. As she fumbled to put on a life-jacket, she became aware that the palms of her hands were burnt, that they were painful. No time to think about that now. Carefully they got down into the small, rocking boat.

While Rafe fitted the oars into the rowlocks, Lilly undid the rope that held them to the jetty, clumsily because her hands were raw. The relief she felt as they pulled away from the jetty, on the black water that was tinged with red, was so strong that she wept silently, still not looking back. If she concentrated on the motion of the boat she could maybe delude herself that they were on holiday. Rafe's unshaven face, his tousled hair, however, made the deception difficult.

As the ribbon of dark water widened between themselves and the jetty, further reaction set in for Lilly. Her hands were shaking as she adjusted her gear around her feet.

Only when they were far out did she dare to look back at the burning town, at the night sky lit up, a quick glance only. Then she concentrated on Rafe opposite her, smoothly, steadily applying the oars. The relief at getting out was tempered by a sense that their skills were needed back there, where the fire trucks would be lined up in a last stand for the town, hosing down what they could hope to save, trying to put out fires that had already started. Yet they were out of their depth, she and Rafe. Now they didn't want to be a liability to anyone.

The scent of smoke followed them as they went. It was good to be alive, to be going to safety in this flimsy craft.

"Hang on, Lilly," Rafe said, after a while, breathing heavily from the unfamiliar exertion. "I'm going to turn now. Watch out for that jetty I mentioned."

# CHAPTER SEVEN

THEY went on in silence, parallel with the shore now, further away from the garish light. Lilly pounding heart was returning to something approaching a normal rate.

The night was humid and oppressive. Carefully, so as not to rock the boat, Lilly eased out of her life-jacket and took off her T-shirt to dip it in the water of the lake. After squeezing it out, she put it on again. ''Ah, that's better,'' she said tremulously. Never would she forget this boat ride on the dark water. It was taking her to a new life, she sensed that with a certainty that was calming.

After a while they could no longer see the actual flames, only the glow in the sky, and then even that diminished, so that they were moving on the still water in a strange grey half-light. Losing all track of time, they pulled away to safety and Lilly fixed her gaze on the silhouette of the man in front of her, on his rippling muscles as he pulled on the oars, soothed by the sound of the water.

After what seemed like a long time, she spotted the jetty projecting out from a wooded area. ''I can see the jetty!'' she said, pointing. ''I think. Not too far away. Time to go in closer.''

Panting from the unfamiliar exertion, they tied up the boat at the rickety wooden jetty and Lilly climbed a ladder up to the top. Squatting down at the top, she reached for the rucksacks and food that Rafe passed up to her. All around them was the quiet of forest and lake, a forest that could also erupt into flames.

They both lay flat on their backs, breathing deeply, their eyes closed, so utterly exhausted that they did not have the energy to speak. Rafe's hand moved to grip hers and she moved so that her arm was against his. This was pure happiness, she knew it then.

They slept side by side, with no sense of time.

When Lilly awoke to the sound of chirping birds she could see the first faint glimmerings of a grey dawn. The damp T-shirt, under the life-jacket, which she had not had the energy to take off, was stuck to her body, she found when she struggled to a sitting position. The weathered boards of the narrow wooden jetty had left her body feeling bruised, yet how great it was to have slept, even for a short while. Reaction and shock set in, and she found herself shivering.

Rafe stirred beside her and sat up, looking even more like a desperado with his unshaven face and wild hair, which she could see only dimly. "You look great with that beard," she said, smiling.

For a long moment they looked at each other and then he reached forward and gently stroked hair away from her face. All around them the forest sighed and rustled in the breeze off the lake and water lapped against the pilings. How innocent and carefree it all seemed here.

"Look at your hands," he said, picking up one of her hands that she was resting in her lap and peering at it closely in the dim light. "They must be painful. You were trying to save me." Gently he brought her hand to his lips and kissed the reddened, sore palm.

"I can bear it. It's so good to be alive," she said quietly, the touch of his mouth on her hand making her want to weep with gratitude that fate had given him back to her, whether it was to be permanent or temporary. She pressed her lips together to stop them trembling.

"You're hurt, too," she said, reaching forward tentatively to touch the skin of his shoulder, not sure whether she really had the right to touch him. "Is it painful?"

"Not very much," he said. "I can live with it."

Lilly unzipped the uncomfortable life-jacket and struggled out of it.

"I have some ointment in a first-aid kit I can put on those hands," he said, helping her out of the bulky jacket.

"Thanks," she said, trembling as his hand touched the bare skin of her neck and stilled there before moving up into her hair. When she half turned towards him, it was a consent of sorts, and with a sigh he drew her into his arms and in a moment his mouth was on hers and his hands easing her damp T-shirt away from her body, smoothing over the skin of her back.

The kiss was fierce and hungry, echoing all the longing that was in her as she responded. Lilly put her hand up into his hair and held him to her. For long moments they clung together, making up for lost time, a desperation mounting in them. Pulling back from her, he lifted her T-shirt over her head and then un-clipped her bra, taking it off.

The air felt like velvet on her bare skin as he pulled her down, her head on the life-jacket, and lay down beside her. She murmured his name as he gently smoothed his hands over her breasts and she clung to him. After the horror of the night, this was an affir-mation of life. Neither of them spoke, there was no need as he undressed her and then himself, easing their clothing under her body so that the hard boards of the jetty would be more comfortable.

In the darkness that was gradually turning to light, they made love with a fierce intensity, making up for all the pain of separation, all the wasted time. Although they were in the open air, it seemed strangely private and intimate there. Lilly welcomed the weight of his body on hers, the familiarity yet the novelty of him. He never ceased to delight her and she clung to him with all the desperation that had come out of the wrongness of her decision to leave him.

They lay entwined, their faces close, his lips touch-ing her cheek.

"What are we to do, Lilly," he murmured, "you and me? For a long time I've been waiting for an explanation from you. Maybe this is the time and place. We have nothing else to do right now except keep ourselves alive."

"Before I lost the baby," she began, not sure exactly what she was going to say, only that she had to tell him, "your stepmother and her mother came to see me and threatened to have you cut out of your father's will. They offered me one million dollars to get out of your life."

There was an incredulous silence from him for a few moments after she had stopped talking. "What? Is that why you moved out?"

"Partly. Not…not for the money, of course. I didn't accept that." She tried to say it calmly. "They frightened me, intimidated me, threatened me—that's partly why I moved out. I also moved out for the reasons I said. I wanted to be alone for a while, to think. They made me feel that I wasn't good enough for you…but, then, I felt that anyway, that you would one day leave me. They just sort of underlined what I thought I already knew. I didn't want you to feel trapped, or be cut off from your father."

"Why didn't you tell me this before?" he said, his hand stroking her face.

"I don't know really, I just couldn't seem to…" Her voice trailed off as she fought her emotions. "I was frightened that what they said was true, that you would perhaps offer to marry me because I was pregnant and because you would want to do the "right thing". They said I had become pregnant deliberately, which wasn't true. Then I went into clinical depression, which I tried to hide. That's always a mistake, I see that now, because you don't get any sort of help. And I sure needed help."

Rafe sighed. "Oh, Lilly, Lilly," he chided her. "You dear, sweet girl. I apologize, with all my heart, for them," he said. "They don't figure in my life, not at all. What they said was a load of rubbish."

"They intimidated me," she said.

"'Not good enough'." He repeated her words. "I'm not sure I know what that means. At one time I guess most people knew what it meant. We are all unique, we each have something to offer."

"Yes."

"I wish you'd told me this a long time ago," he said, raising himself up to look at her, to kiss her.

"Would it have made any difference?" she asked. "You didn't seem overjoyed that I was pregnant, Rafe."

"It would have made a difference," he said. "The day you told me you were pregnant I had just come through a horrendous work experience, I wasn't thinking straight. I'm not super-human, Lilly. I'm vulnerable, just like the next person."

"And now?"

"I don't know."

"I tried to tell you all this before…" She struggled for an explanation. "But then I found that I couldn't. Perhaps I was frightened to have it confirmed that we were not meant to be together. Then it was just easier to get out," she said. "I was—am—so sad. Their verbal attack on me brought back some childhood memories." Briefly, she told him about her father being wounded in the army, of being invalided out, of having little money and having to live in a trailer for a year, of the taunts she had been subjected to at school.

"That's who I am, Rafe. Those events shaped me," she finished up quietly. "I didn't seem able to tell you before. Sometimes when you're a child you feel ashamed of events and circumstances that are not of your making, things that you can't do anything about. They have a disproportionate effect on you."

"I know, I've been there. So we had to come all the way here for you to say that," he said, amazement in his voice. "That seems a bit much, Lilly."

"That's the way it is," she said.

He moved to lie on his back, though their bodies still touched. "Well, you had better know that I'm not exactly brimming over with self-confidence where women are concerned, although it may have seemed otherwise," he said.

"It did seem otherwise," she said. "You always seemed very confident."

"Being in the middle between two parents who both wanted custody in a bitter divorce isn't conducive to that kind of casual confidence,'' he said. ''It was only because I was old enough to have a say in the matter that I got to live with my mother, and not the wicked witch of the west. So you see, Lilly, I do know something about being shaped by childhood events.''

''I do understand. Why me, anyway?'' Lilly said, forcing herself to say the words calmly, although inside she was in turmoil. ''You could have any woman you want.''

''Could I? Is that what they said?'' He gave a cynical laugh. ''Only in theory. Those are the sort of women I don't want, the ones who can be bought.''

''You didn't answer my question,'' she persisted quietly. ''Why did you want me to live with you?''

''I thought I made that clear at the time.''

''You said you loved me, but I wasn't sure.''

''I wanted you because I thought you were sweet, genuine, unpretentious,'' Rafe said.

Sensitive to nuances, she wondered if his use of the past tense was intentional.

''I took you to be a woman of integrity, brave, with the courage of your convictions, in a quiet, unassuming way. I liked that.'' Perhaps it was intentional…

She said softly, ''You have to understand that I'm in a state of mourning. I have this strange sense of loss, which I can't seem to shake off, even though I've tried to get out of it. It seems that I just have to wait, to let nature take its course, or whatever one wants to call it. I…can't think straight. I told you all that before, maybe in different words.''

He put a hand over hers and squeezed it gently. ''All right,'' he said. ''Fair enough. I wanted to help. I had got to the point where I thought you would never call me, or answer my calls.''

''Sorry,'' she whispered.

''I just wanted you to know that if you needed me, I'd be there,'' he said simply.

''Thank you.'' Again, the words came out in a whisper. ''As I said, I wish I could do something to get rid of this sadness, but I can't seem to… I'll just have to wait. Being with you here helps after what we've just been through.''

''In the things that matter, in our values, our philosophy of life, we're very much the same,'' he persisted. ''And I'm more like my mother than my father. My mother refused a lot of the money that my dad wanted to give her, because she wanted to feel and be independent as much as possible, although, as I've told you, she let him pay for my education, and a few other things, because I'm his son. Forget about all that, Lilly. We can put it in the past where it belongs.''

''I wish I could forget it,'' she said. ''I'm trying.''

He leaned over and looked down into her face. More than ever, in the increasing light of dawn he looked like a pirate, and she found herself smiling.

''I love you, fair Lilly,'' he said.

''I love you,'' she whispered back, reaching forward

to touch his face which was so dear to her, and felt a rare peace seeping into her soul, soothed by the lapping of the water. There was a sense in her of living intensely in the moment, that the future would take care of itself. For the first time in ages they were perfectly attuned. And she felt safe. If fire reached them, they had the water.

After a while they dressed, then opened one of the packages of food and munched on sandwiches and fruit and drank water.

When dawn showed them the path, they started to walk through the woods, the darker interior illuminated by Rafe's flashlight. They walked steadily and fast, hand in hand or in single file where the path narrowed. For her part, Lilly's thoughts were partly with the firefighters, then in flashes she thought of her life with Rafe as it had been, their cosy home that they loved, the shared living. From this distance and in this place, it seemed like a paradise.

It was light and bright when they gained the road. Exhausted and aching they sat on the grass beside the road and ate more food and drank deeply from the water bottles.

"I can hear a vehicle," Rafe said, getting to his feet, shoving the remains of their meal into his rucksack.

"It's coming from the wrong direction," Lilly said, as a blue pick-up truck came into view from the direction of the airstrip.

"I'd rather like to go back to Crater Lake to see

what's happening,'' Rafe said, almost casually. ''How about you?''

''Let's do it,'' she said.

The driver pulled over as they waved to him. ''Hi,'' he said cheerfully. ''You look like you've been in a fire.''

''We have,'' Rafe said. ''You going back to Crater Lake?''

''I plan to get as close as I can to it. Got some essential supplies in the back here. They had a bad night of it, so I heard. But the fire has veered away from the town now, to the south, with the wind. The guys are holding things steady there. Jump in.''

''Thanks.'' They squeezed in the front with the diver.

''Are you Dr Neilson and Nurse Page, by any chance?'' the driver asked.

''Yes, we are,'' they replied together.

''There's a doctor, Will Amos, and a nurse, Ashley Soper—I think I've got that right—at the airstrip, and they said if I saw you, to say they couldn't leave without you and will be coming back to town as soon as they can get official permission. Right now, they've got a first-aid post set up there.''

''I had a feeling they wouldn't go,'' Lilly said.

''They must be pretty worried about us,'' Rafe commented. ''And I rather think that World Aid will be mad with us when they know we've deliberately put ourselves in harm's way.''

"We were careful," she said.

The driver dropped them off in a makeshift parking lot on the edge of town where he intended to leave the truck, not far from the boathouse area.

"I'm going to take a look around," he said. "You folks take care. You'd better report to someone in authority. There's a checkpoint just over there. If you need a ride out, there will be people going from here."

"Thanks."

"And if you need a swim, there's a little cove over there, through the trees a ways."

"Thanks. Swim first?" Lilly asked Rafe. "Or shall we take a look at the town?"

"The latter," he said.

Stiffly, exhausted, they walked the short distance to what was left of the small town of Crater Lake.

When they got to the edge of the town where, surprisingly, several tall trees stood untouched beside the road, they stood together, looking at the devastation.

It was odd how fire had destroyed some buildings and not others, leaving the streetscape like a grim mouth where some teeth had been knocked out, while others had remained. They could see a crude pattern, where fire had made inroads among the buildings, then had veered south, sparing others.

Lilly thought of photographs she had seen of the First World War no man's land, denuded of life, churned earth and the bleak stumps of a few trees left standing upright here and there.

"Look, Rafe," she said, "the boathouse is still standing. And someone has set up a first-aid post from the van that we left on the jetty. It survived."

They both burst out laughing with relief. The boathouse, although charred and buckled, was still more or less upright.

The van with the medical supplies was marooned at the far end of the jetty. They could see it clearly from where they stood, as some of the buildings that would previously have obscured the view had burnt down. Debris partially blocked the road that they had escaped down the night before. It looked as though some army medics had set up shop there on the jetty, identified by a red cross drawn on a piece of cardboard.

"Good for them," Rafe said, grinning. "I had a feeling they wouldn't get out. The army doesn't leave its post."

"Not like us," she said. "We're pretty soft. I'm glad all those medical supplies didn't go to waste."

From where they stood they could see a firefighter sitting in a chair, being treated for smoke inhalation beside the van.

They gave their names to a man at the checkpoint, then, as they stood looking around them, a man carrying a shovel came up to them. He was stripped to the waist, wore a pair of tattered shorts, a baseball cap and a pair of fireproof boots. All exposed parts of his body were streaked with soot and liberally sprinkled

with small abrasions, cuts and burns. Lilly found herself assessing him quickly as a patient.

"This was my shop," he said, pointing to a gaping
hole that contained only a charred concrete basement
with debris in it and a brick chimney. All else was
gone. "My home was above it."

"You've lost everything?" Rafe asked.

"Not the things that matter," he said. "We're alive,
all of us, by some sort of miracle…my family, all the
people I love. My neighbours all made it. We saved
our dog and two cats. My kids don't mind losing all
their gear, so long as they've got the animals. That's
brought us all closer together. The other is just stuff.
You can replace stuff."

"Yes, you're right," Rafe said quietly. "It doesn't
matter."

"We got our family photographs and our papers.
My wife went for the family photographs right away
when we knew we only had an hour before we had to
get out. That's our history, isn't it?"

"Yes, it is," Rafe said. "So they let you back, obviously."

"Yes. I've had some experience fighting fires."

They stood for a few minutes, as though to imprint
all this on their memories. Already they knew they
would never forget.

"If you would like to get something to eat," the
man said, gesturing with a blackened hand, "Someone's set up a food booth just down the street there.

Someone brought in some food from the airstrip, so we won't starve. They've even got beer.'' He grinned at them.

"Thanks.''

"I want to thank you people, and all the others, for coming in here to help us. It's been very much appreciated,'' he said. "My name's Vern, by the way.''

They all shook hands. "Very pleased to meet you, Vern,'' Rafe said. Lilly could tell that his emotions were as close to the surface as hers were.

"Likewise,'' Vern said.

"We couldn't do much,'' Lilly said, feeling overwhelmed, dwarfed by what they saw around them.

"Just by coming here, being here, you've helped us…you and the army,'' he said. "We don't feel so alone. Sometimes you feel you're going mad when you look around and see all this, when you think what you've lost. Then you get steadied again when you see all the great people who've come in here to help us. They've come from all over the country…fire crews, soldiers, volunteers. And some from the US as well. It's just amazing, absolutely amazing.''

"You've helped us, too,'' Lilly said, her voice trembling, "by showing us your courage. It's been a maturing experience.'' And I sure needed that experience, she might have added, but didn't, to this man who had lost his home and all his material possessions. It has shown me to myself.

"Must get on,'' Vern said. "You take care, now.''

"And you," Lilly said.

A few minutes later they stood drinking coffee at the booth that had been set up just back from the main street, looking out over the calm water of the lake that shimmered in the sunlight. All around them the shells of buildings smouldered and smoked, while men from time to time came by to douse the worst of them. Lilly thought that she would never get the scent of smoke out of her nostrils.

Rafe put his free arm round her shoulders, drawing her close to him, and she put her arm around his waist. As the man had said, it seemed like a miracle that they still had each other. They belonged together, she knew that now, she and Rafe. Some things were not relevant to that central truth.

"Will you marry me?" he asked casually, not looking at her.

"Yes," she said.

When he had asked her before, she'd thought he was asking out of a sense of duty because she'd been pregnant, and she had thought that maybe she wasn't good enough for him—whatever that had meant at the time—so she had said no. It was time she stopped putting herself down. He wanted her, and she could tell by the tension and uncertainty in his voice that he did not take her for granted, did not take an affirmative answer for granted. Love suffused her like a warm glow that had nothing to do with the increasing heat of the day.

"Are you sure?" he said softly, his tone lightening. There were a few other people around them, getting food and drink. There was an urgency about everything—they could not wait.

"Absolutely," she said, holding him firmly against her, wanting to be close. It was good to feel his warmth, the firm muscles of his waist.

"When?"

"As soon as we get back to Toronto," she said quietly, shyly. "Please. I don't want to wait."

"Consider it done," he said, turning to her, looking into her eyes, giving her that slow smile that she loved and which, combined with his grimy face and matted hair, added a boyish sweetness to what was otherwise a haggard and exhausted face. "If we could find a preacher, we could even get it done here."

Lilly laughed up at him. What she saw in his eyes were love, tenderness, hope and happiness, and she knew that those emotions were in her own eyes as she looked back at him in complete understanding.

"We could even get a dog and a couple of ferrets, if you like," he said.

"You remembered that I like dogs and ferrets! I'm going to make you keep that promise," she said, laughing.

"I want you to."

"We'll honour our commitment to World Aid," she said. "I want to stay here for as long as we're needed.

Even though they will be very annoyed with me for having my 'significant other' on the job with me.''

They laughed at that.

''Agreed,'' he said squeezing her against his body. ''I won't leave here without you.''

''I want to keep it very simple, our wedding,'' she said dreamily, finding that she couldn't stop grinning. ''Just you and me and a few other people. We can tell the world later.''

''Agreed,'' he said again, his voice light with relief and happiness. ''A burnt out church would be pretty simple.''

Lilly offered up a silent prayer that somehow they had come through a dark time, had found each other fully this second time around. There would be no subterfuge, no worrying about not being good enough, or whatever. It was a novelty to feel that wonderful thing again that was happiness.

''I want another baby soon,'' she said shyly, knowing that even now there was the possibility of new life forming inside her. The thought gave her a strange sense of joy. Perhaps by the time they had finished at Crater Lake, if they got to stay, she would know for sure.

''Consider that done, too,'' he said, grinning.

Lilly rested her head against his upper arm. ''I love you. We have so much,'' she said. ''I'll never take anything for granted again.''

''Except my love,'' he said. ''You can do that.''

"Thank you."

"All the days that I have on this earth are yours," he said. "That's what matters, Lilly."

"I'm going to cry," she said.

"Every little bit of water helps here," he said, so that she laughed at the same time.

As they had been standing there, the sky had darkened and the humidity increased. "Looks like rain," the man in the booth said cheerfully. They knew he was one of the local people who had lost all his material possessions. "There's going to be one humdinger of a storm, with rain this time. Better get under cover, if you can find any cover to speak of." He laughed. "Just don't stand under a tree."

When he laughed again at his own joke, they joined in. With that laughter came hope for all of them, hope for the present and for the future. They would both embrace that with open arms, because the way had become clear to them.

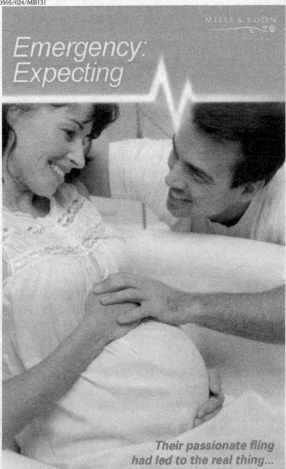

0505/03a

MILLS & BOON®

Live the emotion

# _Medical
## romance™

### THE DOCTOR'S SPECIAL TOUCH by *Marion Lennox*

Dr Darcy Rochester is horrified when 'doctor' Ally
Westruther sets up her massage business next door.
He doesn't think she's qualified, and won't let her put
his patients at risk! He soon learns his mistake. But
why does such a talented doctor refuse to practise
medicine? And why does she want nothing to do
with love?

### CRISIS AT KATOOMBA HOSPITAL by *Lucy Clark*

*(Blue Mountains A&E)*

After a challenging time as a doctor on the frontline, Dr
Stephen Brooks needs somewhere to unwind. Where
better than the tranquil retreat of the Blue Mountains?
But when he meets his stunning new colleague Dr
Nicolette Bourgeois relaxing becomes a little difficult!
Could Nicolette be the one to restore Stephen's faith
in love…?

### THEIR VERY SPECIAL MARRIAGE by *Kate Hardy*

With two beautiful children, a successful job and a
husband whom she loves more than anything, GP
Rachel Bedingfield should have a life to envy. She just
wishes she had more time – for herself and for Oliver.
They just don't seem able to communicate any more…
But their relationship is special – theirs really is a
marriage worth keeping…

## On sale 3rd June 2005

*Available at most branches of WHSmith, Tesco, ASDA, Martins,
Borders, Eason, Sainsbury's and all good paperback bookshops.*

*Visit www.millsandboon.co.uk*

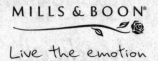

## MILLS & BOON®

*Live the emotion*

# Playboy Lovers

*They're the most eligible bachelors around
– but can they fall in love?*

**In June 2005, By Request brings back
three favourite romances by our
bestselling Mills & Boon authors**

The Secretary's Seduction *by Jane Porter*
The Prospective Wife *by Kim Lawrence*
The Playboy Doctor *by Sarah Morgan*

**Make sure you get hold of these
passionate stories,
on sale 3rd June 2005**

# FREE

## 4 BOOKS AND A SURPRISE GIFT!

We would like to take this opportunity to thank you for reading this Mills & Boon® book by offering you the chance to take FOUR more specially selected titles from the Medical Romance™ series absolutely FREE! We're also making this offer to introduce you to the benefits of the Reader Service™—

- ★ **FREE home delivery**
- ★ **FREE gifts and competitions**
- ★ **FREE monthly Newsletter**
- ★ **Books available before they're in the shops**
- ★ **Exclusive Reader Service offers**

Accepting these FREE books and gift places you under no obligation to buy; you may cancel at any time, even after receiving your free shipment. Simply complete your details below and return the entire page to the address below. You don't even need a stamp!

**YES!** Please send me 4 free Medical Romance books and a surprise gift. I understand that unless you hear from me, I will receive 6 superb new titles every month for just £2.75 each, postage and packing free. I am under no obligation to purchase any books and may cancel my subscription at any time. The free books and gift will be mine to keep in any case.

M5ZEE

Ms/Mrs/Miss/Mr.........................................Initials ....................................
BLOCK CAPITALS PLEASE

Surname ........................................................................................................

Address ........................................................................................................

...........................................................................................................................

..........................................................Postcode ....................................

Send this whole page to:
The Reader Service, FREEPOST CN81, Croydon, CR9 3WZ